THE COMPLETE DELTA FORCE WARRIORS

A MILITARY ROMANTIC SUSPENSE STORY COLLECTION

M. L. BUCHMAN

Buchman Bookworks

PRAISE FOR M. L. BUCHMAN

Tom Clancy fans open to a strong female lead will clamor for more.

— *Drone*, Publishers Weekly

Superb!

— *Drone*, Booklist starred review

The best military thriller I've read in a very long time. Love the female characters.

— *Drone*, Sheldon McArthur, founder of
The Mystery Bookstore, LA

A fabulous soaring thriller.

— *Take Over at Midnight*, Midwest Book
Review

Meticulously researched, hard-hitting, and suspenseful.

— *Pure Heat*, Publishers Weekly, starred
review

Expert technical details abound, as do realistic military missions with superb imagery that will have readers feeling as if they are right there in the midst and on the edges of their seats.

— *Light Up the Night*, RT Reviews, 4 1/2 stars

Buchman has catapulted his way to the top tier of my favorite authors.

— Fresh Fiction

Nonstop action that will keep readers on the edge of their seats.

— *Take Over at Midnight*, Library Journal

M L. Buchman's ability to keep the reader right in the middle of the action is amazing.

— Long and Short Reviews

The only thing you'll ask yourself is, "When does the next one come out?"

— *Wait Until Midnight*, RT Reviews, 4 stars

The first...of (a) stellar, long-running (military) romantic suspense series.

— *THE NIGHT IS MINE*, BOOKLIST, "THE 20 BEST ROMANTIC SUSPENSE NOVELS: MODERN MASTERPIECES"

I knew the books would be good, but I didn't realize how good.

— NIGHT STALKERS SERIES, KIRKUS REVIEWS

Buchman mixes adrenalin-spiking battles and brusque military jargon with a sensitive approach.

— PUBLISHERS WEEKLY

13 times "Top Pick of the Month"

— NIGHT OWL REVIEWS

SIGN UP FOR M. L. BUCHMAN'S NEWSLETTER TODAY

and receive:
Release News
Free Short Stories
a Free Book

Get your free book today. Do it now.
free-book.mlbuchman.com

Other works by M. L. Buchman: *(* - also in audio)*

Thrillers

Dead Chef
Swap Out!
One Chef!
Two Chef!

Miranda Chase
*Drone**
*Thunderbolt**
*Condor**

Romantic Suspense

Delta Force
*Target Engaged**
*Heart Strike**
*Wild Justice**
*Midnight Trust**

Firehawks
MAIN FLIGHT
Pure Heat
Full Blaze
*Hot Point**
*Flash of Fire**
Wild Fire

SMOKEJUMPERS
*Wildfire at Dawn**
*Wildfire at Larch Creek**
*Wildfire on the Skagit**

The Night Stalkers
MAIN FLIGHT
The Night Is Mine
I Own the Dawn
Wait Until Dark
Take Over at Midnight
Light Up the Night
Bring On the Dusk
By Break of Day

AND THE NAVY
Christmas at Steel Beach
Christmas at Peleliu Cove
WHITE HOUSE HOLIDAY
*Daniel's Christmas**
*Frank's Independence Day**
*Peter's Christmas**
*Zachary's Christmas**
*Roy's Independence Day**
*Damien's Christmas**
5E
Target of the Heart
Target Lock on Love
Target of Mine
Target of One's Own

Shadow Force: Psi
*At the Slightest Sound**
*At the Quietest Word**

White House Protection Force
*Off the Leash**
*On Your Mark**
*In the Weeds**

Contemporary Romance

Eagle Cove
Return to Eagle Cove
Recipe for Eagle Cove
Longing for Eagle Cove
Keepsake for Eagle Cove

Henderson's Ranch
*Nathan's Big Sky**
*Big Sky, Loyal Heart**
*Big Sky Dog Whisperer**

Love Abroad
Heart of the Cotswolds: England
Path of Love: Cinque Terre, Italy

Other works by M. L. Buchman:

Contemporary Romance (cont)

Where Dreams
Where Dreams are Born
Where Dreams Reside
Where Dreams Are of Christmas
Where Dreams Unfold
Where Dreams Are Written

Science Fiction / Fantasy

Deities Anonymous
Cookbook from Hell: Reheated
Saviors 101

Single Titles
The Nara Reaction
Monk's Maze
the Me and Elsie Chronicles

Non-Fiction

Strategies for Success
Managing Your Inner Artist/Writer
*Estate Planning for Authors**
Character Voice
*Narrate and Record Your Own Audiobook**

Short Story Series by M. L. Buchman:

Romantic Suspense

Delta Force
Delta Force

Firehawks
The Firehawks Lookouts
The Firehawks Hotshots
The Firebirds

The Night Stalkers
The Night Stalkers
The Night Stalkers 5E
The Night Stalkers CSAR
The Night Stalkers Wedding Stories

US Coast Guard
US Coast Guard

White House Protection Force
White House Protection Force

Contemporary Romance

Eagle Cove
Eagle Cove

Henderson's Ranch
*Henderson's Ranch**

Where Dreams
Where Dreams

Thrillers

Dead Chef
Dead Chef

Science Fiction / Fantasy

Deities Anonymous
Deities Anonymous

Other
The Future Night Stalkers
Single Titles

CONTENTS

About This Book xiii

Introduction xv

LIGHTNING STRIKE TO THE HEART 1

LOVE IN THE DROP ZONE 41

HER HEART AND THE 'FRIEND' 77
COMMAND

PLAY THE RIGHT CARDS 137

CARRYING THE HEART'S LOAD 169

DELTA MISSION: OPERATION RUDOLPH 207

Last Words 257

IF YOU ENJOYED THAT, 259

About the Author 271

Also by M. L. Buchman 273

ABOUT THIS BOOK

Join M. L. Buchman for this six-story companion collection to
The Complete Delta Force Shooters.
Praise for M. L.'s Delta Force series:

- *"The contemporary standard bearer of military romance."*
- *"Top 10 Romance of the Year."*
- *"A romantic adrenaline junkie's kind of book."*

M. L. will lead you on the journey with brand-new introductions to each story, their origins, and why they were written.

Discover tales of danger, adventure, and ever-lasting love with the top warriors anywhere.

Six great reads for one amazing price.

INTRODUCTION

In the first collection, *The Complete Delta Force Shooters*, I included five stories that explored the world of the Delta Force snipers. All Delta Force operators are top shooters, but to be a sniper is a skill above and beyond even the "average" elite soldier.

However, Delta Force, the United States' most elite counter-terrorism team, is so much more than its shooters. They are specialists in undercover work, extraction-and-rescue missions, capture, and even "simple" tracking. Explosives, weapons, infiltration...the list seems unending.

In this collection, I explore some of these other skills as my warriors fight for their lives—and fall in love. For some, the voyage is dangerous and gritty, for others perhaps a little more fanciful.

But I still sought to hold true to my core intent of discovering more about the warriors and their skills.

These may not be the "shooters", but they were certainly both a joy and an education to write.

LIGHTNING STRIKE TO THE HEART

Hal Waldman's next assignment: skydive through a storm into hostile territory. The mission's greatest risk? His own jump partner.

Teresa Mann, on special assignment to assist Delta Force, must make a leap of faith.

Nothing prepares them for when they both take a Lightning Strike to the Heart.

INTRODUCTION

This is the first Delta Force romance story I ever wrote.

I had written twenty-five other stories before I tackled this one. Curiously, that did little to diminish the fear factor of starting a new series, especially one like this one.

Could I capture an entire mission in a short story?

The mission and the romance were at odds. One happens extremely fast, it's Delta Force after all, and the other needs time to grow. How could I possibly combine two such disparate elements?

The excitement and stress of a mission, combined with romance, had its own trap that I wanted to avoid. I didn't want these to be tales of heat and action that would lead to fiery sex (no matter how fun that might be to write) rather than to lasting love.

But as I mentioned in the first collection, I wanted to also show the incredible skills that it takes to belong to the world's most elite military team.

In this story, I focused on the HALO jump. It is

considered to be the most difficult and dangerous parachute jump of them all.

Jumps are often initiated at great altitudes, airliner altitudes. In attempting to avoid possible radar detection, the jumper freefalls for most of that distance at terminal velocity, opening the parachute at the last possible moment.

Potential problems include: frostbite (it can be minus fifty or lower at altitude), straying off target, a late opening means a minimum of time remains to cut away the primary chute and go to the reserve chute if there's a problem... The list goes on at great length. Jumpers can even get the bends if their climb to altitude happens too fast, or the cabin pressure is changed too suddenly, so they have to pre-breathe pure oxygen (a fire hazard) to flush the nitrogen out of their systems.

Of course, it didn't sound like enough fun, so I added a storm. It's just the evil writer that I am.

One thing puzzled me though. Delta Force operators are not held to strict military guidelines regarding grooming. In order to be able to infiltrate various places, they'll often grow longer hair and beards. Some will even take this liberty to extremes, but that wasn't an issue for this story to explore.

However, the challenge of blending in during an infiltration can be easier as a couple. There's the added issue in the Arabic and Muslim world, that women may not touch or directly address men who are not of their family.

So where does Delta Force get their women?

This story was written well before the laws were

changed allowing women to serve in all combat positions in the US military.

I found one obscure reference that they tapped, of all curious outfits, the US Coast Guard. I've since had career Coasties argue that this wasn't possible, but we're talking Delta Force here, so they would have kept it pretty quiet.

Possible or not, I was awfully glad to find Teresa Mann was willing to serve.

1

———

IT WAS A BITTER NEW YEAR'S EVE, ESPECIALLY AT THIRTY-three thousand feet standing on the open rear ramp of a C-130 Hercules cargo plane. The rain drummed on the plane's skin with such ferocity that she could barely hear the roar of the massive turboprop engines over the storm. She had to stay light on her toes to keep her balance on the shifting deck.

Chief Petty Officer Teresa Mann of the US Coast Guard checked her watch: oh-two hundred. Happy New Year. What better time, place, and weather for her first combat jump with a Delta. She'd been thrilled at the chance to accompany a Unit operator—as Delta Force soldiers called themselves—but this was a little extreme even by the Airborne Jumpmaster Course's harsh standards. She'd done HALO jumps before—bail out at high-altitude but wait for the last second before doing a low opening—but not in the middle of the night during a major storm.

The C-130's Loadmaster spoke over the intercom

wired into her earphones, "Jump in fifteen seconds." Only the dull red jumplight lit the cavernous rear of the aircraft. He and his assistant were anonymous in a full helmet and armored vest as the four of them grouped together for their final checks.

Teresa began counting backwards.

"Ground reports winds out of the southwest at forty," he provided the last key element before the jump.

In other words a total nightmare for the landing.

"In ten!" He was a second fast. Then he yanked her and Hal Waldman's communications cables, and her earphones went quiet.

He disconnected their oxygen hookups to the aircraft's supply system.

For a jump from this altitude, she and Hal were wearing full facemasks and carrying five minutes of oxygen. Instead of helmets, they wore insulated caps that fitted tightly against the mask. Five minutes allowed plenty of margin for error as they should fall into breathable air within ninety seconds, but they couldn't risk cracking their masks for the full three minutes of the jump until they deployed their chutes—the chance of getting frostbite from the wind chill was too high. They'd already checked each other head to toe to make sure there was no exposed skin. With a sixty-second margin of air, they were good to go.

The Loadmaster unlatched Master Sergeant Waldman and then her own safety lines that had kept them securely connected to the racing cargo plane once the rear ramp had been lowered.

Then the Loadmaster caressed her ass and gave it a hard squeeze.

Rather than going for the obvious response—a sharp kick to the balls, which he was already turning aside to protect against in addition to having an armored flap dangling over his groin from his bullet-proof vest—she made her hand into a knife edge and drove her fingertips upward into his armpit through the gap in his armor between vest and sleeve. Once there, she grabbed and twisted the leading edge of the pectoral muscle hard enough that his arm wouldn't work right for days without causing a shooting pain down its whole length. She gave an extra yank; he'd walk with a hunch for most of that time.

His hand, which had clutched her even harder in initial shock, finally let go.

As he jerked it back, she brought the edge of her hand down in a hard chop that may or may not have broken his wrist.

By the volume of his scream—which was loud enough to be heard over the roar of rain and engine, despite no longer sharing the intercom—she'd guess a bad break. Hardly a traditional start to the New Year.

She stepped to the rear edge of the cargo ramp with Hal. At the last second Teresa turned so that she was facing the still screaming Loadmaster and his assistant, who was clawing at his headphone's volume control. She snapped to full attention as she stepped off the end of the ramp. With a sharp salute, she drifted off the plane and fell backwards into the storm.

"Any problems?" Hal asked over their short-range

encrypted radio link as they slammed from the plane's two hundred miles an hour into freefall. Once they were flying with the wind, the battering eased.

"It depends Waldman, are you a macho asshole?" In the pitch dark, Teresa oriented herself head down and lined up her body for the fastest descent speed.

"I've been accused of the macho often enough. I try to avoid giving women a cause to call me an asshole though."

"Then we're fine."

2

———

HAL DID HIS BEST TO KEEP ANY THOUGHTS ABOUT CHIEF Petty Officer Teresa Mann's fineness to himself as they plummeted downward through thirty thousand feet and headed toward twenty-five. By that time they had reached terminal velocity. At a hundred-and-fifty miles per hour, the rain wasn't merely noisy, it was also painful as it drove against his jumpsuit like a rapid fire BB gun.

There was no sign of the city that lay below; the clouds had gathered so thickly that no hint of light made it up to their altitude.

He'd seen the Loadmaster's grope and, while he agreed that Mann had one of the best asses he'd ever seen in the military, he'd been trying to figure out how to report the man for his action as there wasn't either time or opportunity for him to step in and thrash the man himself without missing the jump window.

Then Mann had taken action of her own and absolved him from that part of the problem.

The primary difficulty with making a report was that

the C-130's crew had been purposely misled to think that he and Teresa were a couple of crazy CIA spooks being sent in on some intelligence-gathering mission. So no one had asked anyone else's names and no units were mentioned. He and Mann had showed up at the designated place, found the aforementioned aircraft, and climbed aboard without a word.

Sending punishment meant reporting aspects of their mission to sections of the command authority that weren't supposed to know about its existence.

He had to admire the efficiency with which Mann had transferred the burden of explanation onto the Air Force Loadmaster. Now it would be up to him to explain how he'd broken his wrist and couldn't use his right arm properly without saying anything about how it had happened. And if he did talk about the two strangers who had jumped out of his aircraft, he'd be grounded so fast that he'd have to sprint to keep ahead of the dishonorable discharge that would be racing to catch up with him. The authority structure of Joint Special Operations Command wasn't a big fan of soldiers who violated their security clearances.

Despite being Coast Guard, Teresa Mann had used Unit thinking which was still disorienting. Rumor said that the first woman of Delta was out in the field and that another was in the Operators Training Course—even if neither possibility sounded very likely. Petty Officer Teresa Mann was on loan from the U.S. Coast Guard's MSST team—the USCG's special forces. If the anti-terrorist Maritime Safety and Security Team produced any other women as obviously skilled as Mann, he'd be seriously impressed. If they had any more that looked like her, he'd change branches of the service just for the female scenery.

He pulled his arm forward, keeping it close to his body to avoid invoking a mid-air tumble, to check the GPS and altimeter. Twenty thousand feet flashed by and he corrected his flight path ten degrees toward the southwest by briefly bending one knee to raise a foot into the wind. The rain pounded so hard against his plastic facemask that he couldn't have heard her if Mann was shouting for help.

They fell through thick clouds, and despite their suits the wet and the wind chill were severe enough that he'd be shivering if the jump adrenaline wasn't pumping so hard. A bolt of lightning slashed somewhere nearby and for a second he saw Mann in clear outline just a hundred feet away, dressed in pitch black against a background of heavy storm, cloud-lit brilliantly from within. Then they were plunged back into darkness.

It was a glimpse he knew he'd never forget, Teresa Mann as Wonder Woman—no, Catwoman—dressed all in black, flying fearlessly through the storm, and dangerous as hell. He thanked whatever Army god had kicked the extraction assignment in his direction just forty-eight hours ago.

HALO jump to listed coordinates. Escort individual to safety. Zero profile.

Which in Delta-speak meant: "don't be seen, even if you have to kill someone—but don't do that either." He considered possible scenarios based on the limited information. Command would have provided more if they had it, which meant he was jumping into an unknown situation, expected to carry out a barely defined mission, and not to be caught. That's why the mission had come to Delta—no one rocked the unknown like The Unit.

But the best option for keeping low cover on the ground would be a man-woman team, so he'd sent a request up the command chain without much hope. But for all the times that the Army mis-delivered—or didn't deliver at all—this time it had supplied personnel magnificently.

There had been the bewildering moment when the tall brunette with hair falling in soft waves to her shoulder had shown up at Incirlik Air Base.

"Chief Petty Officer Teresa Mann assigned to your detail," she'd dropped a set of transit orders into his lap.

"I didn't—" *ask for a liaison officer,* he almost said, but bit off the words. There was something about how a Special Operations field soldier stood that no one else could match. It wasn't attitude, it was competence. And she had it. His initial thought was to ask her the usual litany of questions when facing an unknown soldier with undefined skills, but then he thought better of it—when the roles were reversed, those questions always just pissed him off. So instead he went with, "What was your last assignment?"

And she'd given him the blank stare of experience with those cool brown eyes that said it was classified and he needed to find himself a new question. It was a good sign that her looks aside, she was one put-together soldier. Factor those in and...he looked down at her orders quickly for a distraction. She had her Master Parachutist Badge and also had the security clearance to know what was and wasn't classified—both key elements to this operation.

Hal had waved her to a seat and started right in on the briefing. As they worked out the final shape of the plan, she'd offered suggestions that showed field experience—not deep field experience, but rough enough to learn important lessons the hard way. Maybe women making it through the Delta Selection process and OTC wasn't such an obscure possibility.

Ten thousand feet. On target.

The next bolt of lightning was so close that he wondered if they were about to be fried in the sky. Not that it would phase Petty Officer Mann. His few lame attempts at getting personal had revealed her near-robotic degree of control and dedication to the service. Gorgeous, but she had a wind chill factor even worse than the storm's.

3

____

Teresa figured that her oxygen reserve had run out prematurely and she was going to have to peel back her mask and risk frostbite, when it occurred to her that she wasn't breathing at all. With a sharp gasp, she sucked in oxygen, and her head cleared.

Eight thousand.

Another breath that tasted of panic. She bit it back hard and forced her next breath to be even and regulated.

That last lightning flash had been so close she could still feel the induced charge across her skin. She'd been staring into the darkness toward Hal Waldman, her brain seeking some confirmation that she wasn't alone in this madness, when the bolt had shocked through the clouds close behind her and revealed him in sharp relief against the storm. The brutal thump of thunder slammed her closer to him and momentarily drowned out both wind and storm.

Closer to him. She knew nothing about him, but he exuded confidence and safety. Even in this crazy jump, she felt as if it was possible merely because he fell alongside her.

She'd worked heavy-duty Coast Guard missions before, but when her commander had offered her a shot at jumping with the legendary Delta Force, she'd leapt at the chance. For some idiot reason she'd thought that three years in the MSST had prepared her for anything, but it certainly hadn't prepared her for this. Jumping in this weather proved that the Delta guys really were as nuts as rumor said—something she'd never quite believed until this moment.

She'd been ready for macho bravura and a dismissive attitude. What she hadn't been ready for was when Master Sergeant Hal Waldman had simply waved her to a seat and started right into the briefing without so much as a hello. Pure soldier, a hundred-percent business. When he'd eventually offered a few openings to friendly conversation, she'd been too surprised to react before he shrugged and moved on.

Even after three years, most of the MSST cadre didn't treat her with such simple acceptance. Women were only a little more common there than they were in Special Operations—as in not at all.

Sergeant Waldman's steadiness had helped keep her own nerves calm. She'd only been assigned to carefully planned missions before, until she'd chafed at the restriction, as if she somehow wasn't good enough. Delta's specialty was the short notice plunge into unknown conditions. Someone was finally trusting her out on the edge...actually way past it. Ice fogged most of her facemask and the wind had bitten right through her flightsuit despite the waterproof materials and thick fleece lining.

Three thousand. Two. At one-five she pulled her ripcord and by one thousand, the black chute opened with a sharp crack and the harness slammed up against her crotch and tried to remove her breasts—standard fare for the ride.

A flash of lightning, more distant this time, revealed Hal Waldman close by and still no sign of the ground. She corrected right, then left to tuck in tight behind him.

The squall blowing out of the southwest at forty knots made for excellent cover, but she couldn't believe they'd actually been crazy enough to jump in it.

A parachute typically landed going under twenty miles an hour; a hard stall at the last second could cut that in half. They were going to be blown backwards while flying full-speed forward. Nothing in her combat training had prepared her for that.

A final glance at the GPS showed that Hal already had them flying into the wind and, yes, they were traveling backwards.

"This wasn't in any of my training!" she shouted at the wind.

"Mine either."

Crap! She'd forgotten that they had an open radio link as long as they were within fifty meters of each other.

"Not exactly a confidence builder, Waldman."

"It's the Army, what do you expect?"

She hadn't expected Master Sergeant Hal Waldman to be understanding, let alone have any hint of humor.

The combination was almost enough to make her bobble the descent.

Unit operators were a tough, manly-men bunch, but with four older brothers she knew how to handle that. A Delta soldier would never admit a weakness, yet Hal had just admitted that he too was riding the hairy edge at the moment and it oddly gave her some hope.

They were below two hundred feet when they broke out of the cloud cover.

Her night-vision goggles revealed a classic upper-middle class Iraqi compound displayed in an NVG's thousand shades of green heat. A high stone wall around a dusty courtyard that was currently a muddy courtyard. Several solid-looking buildings that she hoped they didn't hit. A variety of miscellaneous obstacles.

Too late to do more than pick where they were going to crash land, she let nerves and trained reflexes take over. Rather than stalling the chute to kill forward motion, they kept moving ahead at full flight into the wind...and the wind kept carrying them backward. She had to keep glancing over her shoulder to make sure she was being blown toward a safe landing zone.

In a blur too fast for her mind to record, she adjusted to avoid a parked Toyota pickup, dodged a stone well, and slammed backward into the mud. Their chutes dragged them across the courtyard until they slammed into the perimeter wall together. Once she decided she was alive and opened her eyes, her night vision revealed two cows and a goat that were too startled to do more than stare as they cowered there seeking some protection against the wall.

She, Hal, and their chutes were all tangled together. Hal's arms were pinned to her body by a snarl of nylon paracords and his facemask was pressed hard against hers—their noses practically touching except for the two thin layers of plastic.

Hal struggled briefly but was unable to free himself. He didn't use the opportunity for a quick feel even though his arms were wrapped around her.

Thinking back she was able to reconstruct that at the last moment he'd grabbed her and taken the brunt of the slam into the wall himself in order to spare her, which was damned decent—they'd hit hard. She was winded despite the buffer.

They each managed to pull a hand free and peel off their facemasks now that they were out of oxygen. The rain, so cold and painful at altitude, was a refreshing wash across her heated face. The snarl of the paracord kept their faces only inches apart, but he eased the awkwardness with a smile and joke.

"What do you do for fun when you aren't doing crazy shit like this?"

A cow stepped closer to sniff at them as a slap of wind slammed the stink of cow breath and manure at her.

"Barbeque," she told the cow. "Four older brothers, I'm big on barbeque."

4

———

HAL MADE A QUICK SCAN OF THE YARD AS HE LAUGHED AT her joke. Their arrival had gone by unobserved, which was good as they were still snarled together and he couldn't draw so much as a penknife. Her humor after so dangerous a flight helped steady him as he worked to free himself and pack his chute. And their brief entanglement that had forced him into contact with a number of parts of Petty Officer Mann's body—for which he apologized— he couldn't regret for an instant. Despite flight gear, harness, and a small field pack, it had been impossible to avoid the body he'd sat only inches from for the last twenty-seven hours.

Every curve that he'd so appreciated watching, he now knew was backed up by muscle in the best way possible.

She'd also proven to have a sharp intellect and hadn't panicked during the scariest jump *he* had ever been on. Now it was time to see if her skills played out in the field. He certainly hoped so, because they were in the deep end now. For one, he hadn't planned on landing *inside* the compound itself—if this was the right one. The houses were crowded close together here up against the city walls, the big homes of the wealthy and powerful. Here they were close enough to the country to still have ties and traditions there, like the farm animals in the courtyard.

After untangling himself, Hal was only seconds ahead of Mann on stuffing away his chute, and assembling his HK416 rifle and scope. By unspoken consent they swept the compound from opposite directions. The scopes interfaced with their NVGs and showed no guards, which was odd.

Actually, maybe it wasn't. After the pounding they'd taken in the storm, it seemed mild here on the ground by comparison. By any other standards though it was an awful night—a mush of sleet and freezing rain thick enough to haze the main house and the guard's quarters only a hundred feet away.

His scan also proved that they were in the right place. A pre-storm drone's surveillance had matched the layout which he had memorized during planning.

Inspection complete, he chopped a hand toward the guard's quarters where a dim light showed in the window. They'd all be huddled inside, out of the storm, probably coming out only for hourly patrols.

Hal checked his watch, oh-two-fourteen. If the guards had any common sense, none of them would be any emerging for another forty-six minutes. A single light in one of the windows showed that someone was still awake.

He was ten feet from the door when it swung open.

Crap! Fifteen-minute patrols. Oh-two-fifteen. Oh-two-thirty.

Maintaining his sprint, he drove his shoulder straight into the man's gut. With a grunt he collapsed back into the room with Hal on top of him. He brought the stock of his rifle sharply up against the man's chin who then collapsed into unconsciousness. Since the guard had stepped from the lit room into the darkness, his vision had been compromised. He wouldn't be able to report anything of what or who had hit him.

Hal crouched, tense and alert.

A single lamp. A half dozen chairs. A table with a book set face down on its surface. A door to the right and another to the left. A deafening drum roll of rain drove against the tin roof in sharp gusts.

There was a brush against his shoulder, just enough contact to tell him Teresa was rushing by him on the right side.

Hal rolled back to his feet and eased up to the left-hand door. Teresa turned off the light and the room plunged back into night-vision green.

Poised at the doors, they both pulled out dart guns.

At a shared nod they rolled through the doors simultaneously.

Hal was standing in a tiny barren room with a circular hole in the floor and a brass pot of water for rinsing one's left hand and flushing any waste down the hole. He could see the warmth of a recent handprint on the rim of the bowl and a distinct heat by the hole in the floor. He was in a typical mid-Eastern toilet.

By the time he'd re-crossed the main room and reached the other door, Teresa was already retrieving the four darts that had knocked out the other guards.

"Got the bathroom, didn't you?"

"Yeah, how did you know?"

She pointed at the two doors and said, "No immediate outbuilding equals inside toilet. You won by..." then her grin turned wicked, "...process of elimination."

He groaned.

She held up a hand and when he responded in kind she high-fived it with enthusiasm.

Absolutely his kind of woman.

5

———

"NOW IT GETS INTERESTING."

"Interesting," Teresa did her best to match the Master Sergeant's wry tone. In the last sixteen minutes, she'd: beat up on a ham-handed Air Force grunt, performed a HALO parachute jump through the heart of a squall, spent a few minutes unsnarling herself from the splendidly hard-bodied Master Sergeant—a task she'd found herself curiously reluctant to hasten—and taken down five heavily-armed house guards without having to kill any.

"Interesting" didn't begin to cover it.

This was the kind of mission she'd dreamed of for years. Military parents bred military kids and it was finally her turn. It wouldn't last. By tomorrow she could be back at MSST which was far more about training and being ready than action, but for now she'd dive in headfirst.

Again, a careful scan of the grounds from the guardhouse door.

No action.

They swept across the yard to the main house.

Their target obviously wasn't a man prone to worrying. He maintained only minimal guards with only one at a time on night duty patrol. She and Hal had planned for much more security when they were designing the mission.

The front door was locked. Rather than breaching it, Hal signaled her left as he circled right. No hovering. No protecting the "fragile female." In the Master Sergeant's world you were either a soldier or you weren't. It was like a breath of fresh air. No man except her dad had ever believed in her like that.

Side of the house was clear.

At the rear, the only person she encountered was Hal coming around the other way. There were two more goats sleeping in the protection of the narrow space between the stone-and-mortar house and the compound's concrete rear wall, but Hal stepped by them so carefully they barely woke. A powerful soldier who could move so lightly; he was oddly beautiful to watch—part dancer and part walking death.

There was no door, but there was a window. Locked.

Through the glass they could see the clear heat signature of a couple lying together in a bed. She and Hal shifted to another window, smaller and higher.

"I'll boost you up," Hal knelt and cupped his hands.

"No. Me." She had an idea, saw the opportunity, and didn't give him a choice. She knelt quickly with one knee in the slush and the other raised. With her boot firmly planted, her knee would make a solid step for him.

He shrugged, stepped on her knee, balanced a moment to spread tape on the glass. He waited for a renewed blast of wind from the storm and punched it with a gloved fist—the tape prevented any shards from falling to shatter loudly on the interior floor—then he reached through and unlocked it. In moments his weight was gone.

She called up softly, "You in the shitter again?"

6

———

Hal sighed.

Nothing got past Teresa. Not only had he been set up, but he'd climbed right into it without thinking.

He was indeed standing in the master bathroom. A far nicer version than the one in the guard's quarters with a modern shower, a sit-down toilet, and tile work that was probably attractive but was all a uniform dark green, almost black with lack of heat in his NVGs...but still "in the shitter again."

Teresa handed through her rifle, then with a jump-and-grab, slipped through the window and landed beside him. She applied a friendly nudge in the ribs, that lost him about half his air, and then they moved forward into the house. A quick scouting revealed that it was unoccupied except for the master bedroom; they met again outside the closed bedroom door.

No noise or light within.

Hal pulled out a fiber-optic viewer and slipped it

under the door. Both figures still lay on the bed, neither appeared to have moved.

At his nod, Teresa opened the door, while he remained low by the floor with his weapon raised.

One of the figures sat up, a woman with long hair and a heavy nightgown. She turned to face them. "You're early," she said in passable English. "What are you doing here?"

Hal had wanted to keep this mission as low profile as possible, so when the Air Force had a flight already planned that would only need a small route diversion, he'd taken it, adjusting the "preferred" schedule that had accompanied the mission details to match the Air Force's.

The man stirred slowly.

Hal spotted the AK-47 leaning against the wall within easy reach. He moved so that he stood between it and the man who came awake with a start. The man reached for the rifle and shouted in alarm when his hand ran into Hal's thigh in the dark.

"Who are you? What are you doing here? I am just a businessman, but I have friends." The man's voice rose until he was shouting in Arabic.

"I think," Teresa said softly over the radio, "that the man we're looking for is a woman."

The man rose and struck out at him. His fist landed squarely against the butt of Hal's Glock 17 handgun that he wore at the center of his gut for a faster draw. The man yelped as he jerked back his injured hand.

7

———

"ANOTHER HOUR," THE WOMAN INSISTED, "AND I WOULD have been standing out in the yard."

"We're here now," Hal snapped.

Irritation was another new emotion in Teresa's catalog of unexpected sides to Hal Waldman. Accepting a woman without question, not caught staring at her too often, a sense of humor, and now irritation—proving that he actually did have emotions. What else was hidden behind the Master Sergeant's all-business tough-guy mask?

Of course, she'd be irritated too if she'd had to subdue the man in his own bed. Neither the gag nor having his hands and feet bound had silenced him; that had taken Hal resting the barrel of his HK416 rifle against his chest and flicking off the safety.

"What does it matter, lady? Let's get moving before your guards wake up."

Which shouldn't be for two more hours with the dose Teresa had shot into them.

The woman shifted uncomfortably.

Teresa had spent the last year in forward language support for Special Operations Forces working as trainers and advisors in Syria—one of the reasons she'd been so close to hand when the mission call came. Her best friend in high school had been from Egypt, which had influenced Teresa to learn Arabic and spend her Junior Year Abroad in Cairo. The last year in theater had polished her vocabulary and accent.

It had also taught her that many Iraqi women, no matter how Westernized, were uncomfortable talking directly to a man.

"You may speak to me," Teresa remained with English as that was the language the woman had been using.

"If you had taken me when you were supposed to, my husband would know nothing. He would remain in his business and I would be able to deliver all of his passwords to you without him any wiser."

"Don't you think he would have guessed?"

The woman looked over at her husband in a way that required no knowledge of language to translate between two women of any culture.

Teresa glanced at Hal. He hadn't missed the look either. Every attempt she made to pigeonhole him failed miserably. Macho Delta operators weren't supposed to understand when a woman knew they were the brains behind the successful man.

"Why would we want his passwords, but not him?" Hal asked.

The woman continued to stare at Teresa as if Hal didn't exist.

Teresa wondered quite how that was possible. By the glow of the single bedside light—that faded and flickered deeply with each blast of the outside storm—Master Sergeant Hal Waldman looked every inch the conquering hero.

"Because," the woman replied softly, "his business is communications. He designed the secure communications system between Taliban cells throughout the region."

8

———

Their exfiltration plan had included one cooperative male extractee: not a woman and a very unwilling man. Hal had been puzzling over how to adapt to that when Teresa hit the solution.

Now they were all piled in the family Toyota Highlander. The women were both in the backseat, fully covered by robe and veil. The man was in the driver's seat, convinced to behave by the HK416 pressed into his ribcage from inside Hal's own voluminous robe and veil.

"How do you see while wearing this?" The narrow slit at his eyes, covered by a fine mesh to block any view in, might be ideal cover but every time he moved his head what little view he had disappeared behind some fold of fabric.

"Careful," Teresa warned him, "or we'll make you wear nylons for a day. And don't think I can't make you do it."

There wasn't a chance she'd succeed, but he'd wager it would be fun if she tried.

The other woman laughed aloud, then the sound was suddenly muffled as they rounded a corner and pulled up to a military checkpoint.

With a careful prod of the HK, the man behaved.

To Hal's ear he didn't have the proper amount of complaint in his tone for being on the road at three in the morning to drive his wife and sisters to aid a sick aunt in the next town over.

Teresa leaned forward and whispered something in the man's ear. His voice faltered, then he found his stride and they were soon pulling away from the checkpoint. Soon, they were rolling down an empty stretch of highway.

Hal pulled out a satellite phone and dialed the number he'd been given. Twenty minutes later there was a roar close overhead as if the storm, which had been abating, was now hammering back down on them.

Then in the headlights, he could pick out an all-black Night Stalkers Chinook helicopter landing in the middle of the road with its rear ramp down.

They drove straight aboard. After some jockeying, the Loadmaster signaled for lockdown and they were tied into place. They were aloft within two minutes of the helicopter's arrival.

"Let's switch seats and I'll tie him back up."

"Oh, he'll behave," Teresa said with utter confidence.

"What makes you say that?"

"I told him what I'd do to his manhood with my knife if he didn't do everything perfectly. I gave him every reason to believe me."

Even if the man didn't speak any English, he was

glancing over at Hal nervously as if guessing the conversation and seeking protection.

Hal grimaced in sympathetic pain. "Maybe I won't take your nylons bet."

"Pity," a woman's voice spoke from close beside him. The Loadmaster—a woman—was leaning against his lowered window. "I bet you'd look cute in them."

She walked away, humming the tune to a Gypsy Rose Lee stripper song.

"Not a chance," he called out after her, but she just broke into song. Strangely enough the other members of the Chinook's crew joined in as they banked hard, racing back toward friendly territory.

He turned back to face Teresa in the backseat, "Not a chance."

But he sure wouldn't mind seeing Chief Petty Officer Teresa Mann in a pair—a flawless soldier with an amazing body. That was a deadly combo indeed.

*H*AL *DIDN'T SEE ANYTHING* OF *T*ERESA *M*ANN *AFTER THEIR* first few minutes back on the ground. By the time he'd gone through debrief and delivered his two charges, she had faded into the dawn and was already gone back into whatever invisible Coast Guard fog bank she'd popped out of.

Searching for her hadn't helped, not that his operational tempo allowed a lot of time to do so.

An inquiry to MSST was returned with a: *The United States Coast Guard does not respond to requests for information about the Maritime Safety and Security Team.*

A follow-up to the USCG itself simply addressed to CPO Teresa Mann was returned with the puzzling endorsement: *No longer with the service.*

A Google search returned 23,880 hits, and none of them were her as far as he could tell—except for a seriously cute high school yearbook photo from some unpronounceable high school in Poughkeepsie, New York.

Pounding his head against the wall hadn't helped either.

By mid-summer he'd decided that he would give it one more shot. He'd been rotated back to Fort Bragg, North Carolina for some Unit refresher training. He didn't even know where to begin to look for her now that he was stateside, but there had to be some lead he could pick up. If not, he promised himself he'd stop being pitiful about a woman he'd known barely thirty-six hours six months ago...and he'd do that very soon.

The squad he'd spent a long day simulating room-clearing with dragged him out on the town. Hal wasn't really in the mood for some dive bar, but you just didn't turn down seven other grunts who'd fired a thousand rounds each together.

They were three bars into Bragg Boulevard before he gave in and just went with the flow. Tomorrow was a "dark" day—an actual, honest-to-god, stateside day of rest. By the fifth bar they were down to three others plus himself. The other four had been peeled off by some of the bar bait with long legs and bottle-blond hair that always flowed around Fort Bragg.

At the seventh bar, he ended up alone. Hal kind of remembered the other three saying they were moving on, but he'd ground to a halt here. He wasn't drunk, hadn't finished a whole beer in any of the places, but he was slowing down.

An hour later and half a beer in, he wondered if this was where he'd be sleeping tonight. It was a good spot: back in the corner, a band that was just loud enough to turn his brain into tapioca pudding without beating him to death, and a pleasant enough flow of female scenery to keep him entertained. None of them really grabbed his attention but they were fun to watch. And none bothered to gun for the solitary drinker in the corner. When on assignment he usually slept in far worse places.

He knew how he must look. The slight shell-shock of someone fresh back from the front suddenly surrounded by the bounties of America. Unless they were one of your buddies, you just left guys like him alone until they were back up to speed.

The room shifted.

The noise level didn't change.

But there had been something. It was the sort of thing that only a trained operator would probably notice; the *feel* had altered.

He started hunting for the source and it didn't take long to spot. Nine new arrivals—soldiers who moved like operators. But it wasn't just that they were Special Ops; you couldn't get a drink within fifty miles of Fort Bragg without running into some form of top soldier.

Hal blinked a couple of times to bring them into sharper focus.

It wasn't just that they were Delta, though they were unquestionably from The Unit.

There was also a strange energy about them, as if every step they took was suddenly their first.

A new class had graduated from the Operator's Training Course. Nobody else moved that way; that impossible bravado generated by finally knowing that for a fact, you are one of the very best warriors on the planet.

There was an electrical charge that sizzled off their every step.

He should go over and buy them a round, but he hated giving up his corner table.

He should...

A tenth soldier walked in, moving with that same impossible confidence.

The only woman among them, he'd know her anywhere even though her hair was shorter, because only one woman possessed the finest ass in the military.

And when she turned and spotted him? That smile lit him up like one of those lightning bolts had finally caught him.

That's why she'd disappeared off the grid and out of MSST; she'd gone for Delta Selection and made it through the six months of OTC.

He could feel the smile on his own face. Unit Operator Teresa Mann looked as if she too had been struck by lightning and it looked damn good on her.

LOVE IN THE DROP ZONE

Cindy Sue Chavez rocks Delta Force training. However, this time the instructor drives her more than a little crazy. Almost as crazy as being called Cindy Sue.

Master Sergeant JD Ramírez believes in pushing his squad, male or female, as hard as he pushes himself. But Cindy Sue? Her he pushes the hardest of all.

When the mission calls for the sharpest Delta Force can offer, they discover Love in the Drop Zone.

INTRODUCTION

This tale perhaps belongs in the sniper anthology, but as all Cindy Sue shoots is a metal target, it seemed more appropriate here.

As far as I can tell, all Delta Force operators must be more than just exceptional shooters. They have to go through an intensive sniper training.

There are two major and distinct skill sets involved here. Or perhaps three.

One is the actual shooting. Firing accurately over great distances is an incredibly challenging task.

At a thousand yards, a standard round travels for over a second. (The world record kill made in 2017 traveled over four seconds to kill its target 3.5 kilometers away.) In that time and distance, wind can blow it aside, cooler-denser air can cause it to slow and fall more, even the Coriolis effect of the Earth's spin can have an affect.

This last may seem odd, until you realize that the Earth is spinning at a thousand miles an hour at the equator and zero at the poles. When firing to the north or south, the shooter and the target are actually spinning at different speeds—even if they are just a mile apart. A difference of almost two feet per second if directly north or south.

I explored much of this in the first Delta Force novel, *Target Engaged.*

In this story I wanted to look at the second (and third) challenge that a sniper faces—getting there (and getting away afterward).

They must arrive in a position to take out the target without being detected. *And* they must be in such a place that they can also remain undetected after they've taken out their target.

Of course, Cindy Sue Chavez finds a solution that's entirely her own.

1

A shadow loomed over her, blocking out the heat blast of the early morning sun striking across Fort Bragg, North Carolina's Range 37 training area. No question who it was—he blocked out everything good about the quiet morning. Even the chatty cuckoos and the dive-bomber buzz of passing hummingbirds seemed to go silent in his presence.

"Staff Sergeant Cindy Sue Chavez."

"Yes, Master Sergeant JD Ramírez?" Could the man be a more formal pain in the ass? She hated being called Cindy Sue and he damn well knew it, but it wasn't a good idea to talk back to a superior rank—not even when he was being a superior asshole.

Her mother, coming from Guadalajara, had thought Cindy Sue sounded American. But Cindy was Bangor, Maine born-and-buttered and no one in Bangor was named Cindy Sue because it was just too ridiculous—doubly so with her Mexican features and long, dark hair. Her parents had slipped across the border as two starry-eyed sixteen-year-olds seeking the American Dream. They hadn't known any better, but it still rankled. She sighed. America wasn't big on giving out guidebooks to help immigrant dreamers along the way. She should damn well write one, at least on how *not* to name your kids.

Cindy's personal mission to eradicate her middle name had been a success with most of her fellow Delta Force operators. Being a woman in Special Operations did have a few perks. Women were a rare commodity inside The Unit, as well as a reminder of home, most grunts were inclined to treat her nicely and drop the "Sue" after the fourth or tenth time she asked. A rifle butt in the gut often helped the slow learners.

She wasn't about to try that on Master Sergeant JD Ramírez whose dark eyes followed her every move. He positively relished how much she hated her extended name, but he was far too dangerous to risk attacking, at least directly. She loved Mama, so rather than indulging in a bit of matricide for giving her the name in the first place, she was leaning very strongly toward offing Master Sergeant JD Ramírez—from a safe distance.

The heat on Range 37 was already climbing toward catastrophic despite the early hour. Low trees struggled upward to either side of this section of the range. Today's training course lay along the low grassy hillside with scattered scrub and dotted with cheery flowers in yellows, blues, and purples. No hint of real shade anywhere.

Ramírez wore boots, camos, and a tight black t-shirt that had clearly been thought up for men like him. He wasn't exactly Mr. Handsome, but if it was what lay under the clothes that counted, he had Mr. Buff down. His skin had the same liquidy perfect genetic tan as hers, blemished by only a few visible battle scars that served to enhance the image. She'd never dated another Latino and—

Crap!

Some psychotic, "Cindy Sue" personality needed her head examined if she was thinking that about the master sergeant.

The fact that he was a Delta Force instructor standing on a Fort Bragg practice range—perfectly in his element —did help the image right along but she wasn't dumb enough to fall for any girlie, daydreaming trap. Master Sergeant JD Ramírez was magnificent in more than just his looks. He was a hundred percent superior *soldier*. That was what she aspired to. Which was ridiculous for a woman half his size, but it didn't matter. She'd known JD almost as long as she'd been in Delta Force and he was the finest warrior she'd never fought with. They had yet to be assigned to an action team together—merely "rubbing shoulders" in situations like this refresher training.

Ramírez still hadn't spoken, but she was going to wait him out. She wasn't even going to give him the satisfaction of looking up at him. Instead, she began preparing for the day.

His boots took a step away. Hesitated, then took another, unveiling the sunrise's full glare. None of the birdsong she'd been enjoying returned. His attitude had cleared the entire zone.

"Do me a favor," his voice was rough.

She squinted up at him. All she could see was sun dazzle, but she knew from experience that he never quite looked at her when speaking.

"What, Master Sergeant?" *Not choke you to death for being a personal thorn in my backside?* That was almost too big a favor to ask. And why was he haranguing her rather than the other seven operators sitting in the dirt and gearing up to survive today's test?

JD had been on her case since the first moment of the course. She didn't expect him to ease up just because she'd survived her first six months in Delta, hunting Indonesian pirates, but it was way past just being a "thing." His *un*-favoritism was so blatant that the other operators had unwound from their arrogant male smugness of innate superiority enough to comment on it. None had offered to protest on her behalf, of course, but that was fine. As a Delta operator she could take care of herself.

And JD Ramírez was now topping her list of things to be taken care of. Not in a good way. She'd start by stuffing his head inside The Foo Fighters kicker drum. Then have Beyoncé strut her stuff up and down his back while wearing her gold-flecked spike-heel boots. If only.

Today was the final sniper stalking test. It was the last day of a month-long skills refresher. Not a lot of field stalking involved in hunting Indonesian sea pirates. Her shooting precision from a moving platform like a boat or helicopter had certainly been honed, but Delta didn't believe in letting *any* skills go stale. If that meant every deployment ended with a month under the ungentle thumbs of the trainers—who were fellow operators—it was fine with her.

But she was getting a real antipathy for that trainer being JD.

"Don't fuck up, Cindy Sue," he finally managed to grunt out.

"Thanks, Master Sergeant. That's *real* helpful." She didn't need advice on how to get through today's sniper stalking test—especially not from JD Ramírez. She wished she had a few rounds in her rifle to deal with him. Maybe pepper the dirt as his feet to make him dance to *her* tune.

"I'll be your spotter."

Perfect! "Yes, sergeant. Glad it'll be you." So perfect that if she had a spare live round, she just might shoot herself in the foot to get out of it. She could feel the other seven of her teammates risking glances at the friendly little tête-à-tête she was having with the master sergeant. Why wasn't he giving *them* any beef? They'd been working quietly together, preparing for the day.

In stalking tests, spotters were definitely not the helpful guy looking over your shoulder and calling out range-to-target, wind speed, temperature, and all of the other factors required in long-shot marksmanship.

She'd aced the shooting part of the course days ago.

Now, his job was to sit in the target's position with a high-powered scope and try to spot her crawling through the brush to kill him—with a single round. If he could pick her out, catch her even bending a stalk of grass the wrong way, she'd flunk the test and have to start over.

Three fails and she'd be bounced back to a full week of stalker training.

In other words, not a chance was she going to let *anyone* spot her. Especially not Mr. Perfect Soldier JD Ramírez.

She continued preparing her ghillie suit. An itchy mesh of burlap and tattered string, it broke the unnatural shape of a sniper slithering toward their target. Once interwoven with local flora, it would drape like a cloak over her head and body, making her into a small patch of slow-moving landscape. An extension of the ghillie would wrap around her rifle. She began lacing in bits of foliage that were native to this particular range. New Jersey tea and sweetfern grew well here. A small selection of the summer grasses, even now shifting from flexible green to August brittle brown, would add to the suffocating layer she'd be spending the next four to five hours underneath.

There was a certain...stench to a well-prepared ghillie suit. It reeked of everywhere it had been. Dragging it along a dirt road for a 10K run had impregnated it with Fort Bragg dust and grime. Trips through reeking mangrove swamps, snorkeling across cow manure ponds, and crawling up the insides of large sewage pipes had added their own head-spinning miasma of awful.

The Marine Scout Sniper Course had a "pig pond" to teach their snipers to go through *anything* to reach the target. The Delta trainers were far less kind. The old Maine saying, "Cain't get the'a from he'a" simply wasn't in a Delta vocabulary.

Ghillie suit smell never truly washed off the skin

considering the number of hours they'd spent wearing them. The scent clung until at least a couple of layers of skin had been shed over time. It worked as a high-quality male repellent in any bar—certainly better than Deet against the avaricious mosquitos of the Maine woods on her parents' farm.

The smell formed an impenetrable barrier to anyone —except for a fellow sniper. To them it was the sweet stench of belonging. However, repelling all would-be boarders wasn't much of an issue after the first day into the refresher course. Delta training schedules didn't leave much spare time in an operator's schedule. Going to the bathroom. Maybe. Eating? On occasion. Sleep? Yep, sleep was for SEALs and other lazy-ass wimps.

She sat cross-legged in the hot sun and continued working on preparing her ghillie. She did her best to ignore Master Sergeant JD Ramírez as he glared down at her.

There had been a synergy between them since the first day—an unacknowledged one. She never shot as well as she did when JD was watching her. There was something about his mere presence that drove her to be better. At first, she'd hoped that he'd eventually notice the woman inside the soldier.

After the last thirty days, she figured she could do with a lot less "notice."

2

———

JD did his best to look away from Cindy, but it wasn't working. He had a full, eight-operator squad that he'd been hounding through the course for thirty days. Just as planned, they now looked battered and weary. They were completely in that head-down, whatever's-next-bring-it-on mode that every Delta operator knew to their very core. The battle was mental. The course was partly a skills refresher, but mostly a reinforcement that mere human limitations weren't a part of being Delta.

At least he had seven of them in that mode.

Number Eight, Cindy Sue Chavez, sat calm and collected in the blazing sun, plucking up the local plants for her ghillie as if she was collecting a wedding bouquet. Nothing he or the other instructors had thrown at her made her fade in the slightest. Hell, *he* was exhausted.

Delta instructors didn't slack off—they were on rotation, in from field operations as well. If the squad did a mile swim wearing boots, ammo, and a heavy rifle, the instructors swam right beside them wearing the same gear. His shoulders still throbbed from yesterday's ten-mile hike with a forty-pound rucksack, just before the last test day on the shooting range—an exercise designed to rate ability to shoot after a hard infiltration. He was just glad it wasn't his day to crawl across the field hoping to god that some sharp-eyed spotter didn't pick him out of the foliage and send his sorry ass back to the start line.

"What is it about me that you hate so much, Master Sergeant?" Cindy didn't look up from preparing her ghillie suit. Her voice was a simple, matter-of-fact, want-a-soda tone.

"Hate? What makes you think I hate you, Chavez? No more than the next operator who slacks off."

It earned him a single long look from her dark brown eyes before she turned back to preparing her ghillie.

Yeah, they both knew she hadn't been slacking off and he'd been chapping her ass.

"Just don't screw up today." He walked away before he could say something even lamer.

Delta women were rare, but he'd worked with a number of them and was past being gender-biased in either direction. Except Cindy Chavez belonged in a gender all her own. Delta women were tough, real hard chargers, just like the men—Delta Force didn't recruit anyone who wasn't exceptional.

But there was something about her that blew all his calibrations about operators.

Was it her beauty? The fact that she was a top athlete? The fact that she didn't take shit from anyone—not even him? He especially liked that about her.

He hadn't even been able to think of another woman

since he'd first met her over a year ago. It had certainly cut down on his favorite recreational pastime. He'd look at a bar babe with her bright blues and deep cleavage zeroed in on him, and then picture the slender, dark-eyed Cindy Chavez and he was outta there.

Even now he could feel those thoughtful, unrevealing eyes tracking him as if he was her next sniper target.

He walked over the broad, kilometer-long hillside slope that she would be crawling across. It was as ugly as a Kansas prairie—a place he hadn't been able to leave fast enough. He took his seat on the raised platform for the spotter/target—last of the three to arrive. Open to all sides, it had a wooden roof that seemed to focus the heat, even if it blocked most of the sun. From the central rafter dangled a metal target that the snipers would have to hit in order to pass—hit without being spotted.

There wasn't a breath of air. No wind to mask the sniper's traverse through the grass and brush. None that would get in his lungs after standing so close to Cindy Chavez and watch her fine-fingered quick movements of preparing her ghillie.

JD hoped that she made it, he really did. He knew he'd pushed her harder than any of the others. But his next assignment badly needed a woman of Cindy's caliber if they were going to survive it.

3

─────────

A THREE-HOUR SKULL-DRAG ACROSS THE FIELD. *Never bring your head up. Never move two inches when one would do.*

Four of the eight stalkers had been picked off by the sharp-eyed spotters. They'd have another try at it after lunch—by which time the North Carolina heat would be beyond brain-baking and their limbs would already be weary beyond functioning from their first attempt. Fine motor control would be out the window.

Not her.

A Marine Scout Sniper had to start a thousand meters out and crawl undetected to within three hundred meters from the spotter/target. A Delta operator was supposed to get within a hundred: the length of a football field from the best spotters in the business. A fifteen-second sprint away.

The first of the snipers to reach the start line undetected just fired off a blank to indicate he was ready. The three spotters on the platform all focused on finding him. She'd bet it was "Grizzly" Jones. His beard was as unruly as a bear's, which was a fair description of his body shape as well. He was incredibly good.

If the spotters couldn't find him, they'd clear him to fire a single live round at a metal target hanging over their heads. If they still couldn't find the shooter by muzzle flash, or by the blowback suppressor stirring up the grass, then he'd pass the test.

The rule was: no one else moved while they waited for a sniper's second shot.

They were unable to find the shooter. The spotters cleared him to fire.

Cindy heard the hard crack of his live round followed almost instantly by the sharp clang of the metal target mounted in the center of the spotter group.

The spotters continued their efforts, but miscalled his location by a good three meters. A sniper not only had to arrive invisibly, he was also supposed to avoid being shot immediately after making his own kill.

The sniper rose on the all clear signal. She didn't bother wasting time to see who it was.

One thing she'd learned about Delta, rules were for other people.

Since the moment everyone's attention had focused on finding Grizzly—or whoever—Cindy had been headed sideways.

4
—————

Two more snipers had passed. That meant there was only one left and JD would be damned if he could find her.

The time limit was fast approaching and he didn't want Cindy to time out. He needed her on his next assignment. He wanted this success for her. He wanted her—

The thought petered out there. An unfinished truth.

He rubbed the sweat from his eyes. The air was shimmering at even a hundred meters. The smell of baking grass, scrub, and the unique blend that was Fort Bragg dirt—that he knew so well from crawling across so much of it himself over the years—was distracting him.

What would Cindy smell like? Not in her ghillie, but instead fresh from a shower after a hard day in the field? Or still hot and sweaty, lying back among the five-petaled wood-anemone? He liked that thought. It made a pleasant companion as he returned to scanning the field.

The controls on the tripod-mounted scope nearly burned his hand with the late morning heat.

He figured it was okay to think such things, as long as he never showed them. To keep such thoughts about her in check—which was damned hard because she was so incredible—he made a point of keeping her angry at him. Her name had been but the latest of many techniques, but already she was growing immune to it. He was running out of ploys to avoid thinking about her.

Focus on the hunt.

A sniper wasn't just a hunter who could kill at a distance, they were also a countersniper. The very best snipers hunted other snipers. Finding a sniper hunting *him* was eerie...and fun. How he'd stumbled into the best job on the planet, he didn't know. How a woman like Cindy had charged into it simply awed him. He *knew* how goddamn hard it was.

Did that stalk of yellow lupine waver with the blurring heat, or because Cindy had brushed against it? Or was it a part of her ghillie suit? He wouldn't put it past her to put a bright flower in her camouflage, simply because no one else in their right mind would think to do something so likely to draw attention.

Was the dark spot at the right edge of the field and a hundred and twenty meters out just a dark spot in the foliage, or was it the bore of Cindy's rifle aimed his way? There was no glint of the glass of her rifle scope immediately above the dark spot, so he moved on.

There was a directionless snap of someone firing a blank round.

It had to be Cindy, she was the only one left out there.

He double-checked his watch. One minute inside the time limit, she was still good. Knowing her, she'd probably been in position for an hour and had simply waited to make him worry.

A glance down the line at the other two spotters. Neither one had a clue.

He felt an itch between his shoulder blades, but couldn't pin it down.

He called out, "Clear to fire."

All three of them had their heads up from their scopes hoping to spot the muzzle flash. Typically, they could pin down the shooter's location within a dozen meters before the shot, then used the scopes to pinpoint for the muzzle flash. Not this time.

Her second round slapped into the metal target. The other two trainers were still scanning the field.

JD glanced up at the battered metal target dangling over their heads and couldn't help smiling. A thousand rounds had scarred the front of the metal plate. There was only one impact splash on the *back* of the target.

He turned to look behind him. He should have trusted that itch between his shoulders.

A quick scan told him that there wasn't a chance that he was going to spot her—there was a line of dense brush behind the spotter's platform.

The other two spotters noted the direction of his gaze. Their protests about the trainee leaving the boundary of the stalking field were immediate, but he didn't bother listening.

He might not be able to see her, but Cindy Sue Chavez was exactly what he was looking for.

5

———

IN THE LAST TWELVE HOURS, CINDY STILL HADN'T GOTTEN over JD's knowing smile. It had been erased by the time she was called "clear" and had descended from an exceptionally prickly hawthorn tree she'd climbed into on the wrong side of the range.

There's been no hint of a smile as he'd ordered her to prepare for immediate deployment.

"We have an assignment," he'd addressed her without the derision that had become his standard *modus operandi* these last thirty days. "Deep infiltration. High risk. Masquerading as a couple. Minimum time is anticipated as thirty days. If it goes right, we may be deployed for several months together. You're my first choice and my only choice. We'll leave at sunset. Does that work for you?"

Deep undercover with Master Sergeant JD Ramírez? Not the pain in her ass that he'd been for the retraining, but rather the most impressive and attractive soldier she'd ever met—suddenly addressing her as an equal?

Her surprise was vaster than the hundred and thirty acres of the Range 37 shooting range and she'd barely managed to nod her agreement.

At sunset, they'd hustled aboard a C-17 Globemaster transport jet and staked claim to the steel decking of the sloped rear ramp—one of the most comfortable spots on an uncomfortable plane. It had turned southwest toward Mexico and he had done what all Spec Ops warriors did on a flight—passed out. Headed into a mission, you never knew when you'd get to sleep next, so the jet engine's conversation-ending roar worked better than a general anesthetic on any Special Operations warrior.

Except it didn't for her this time. Maybe it was because she'd spent six months deploying from helicopters; sleeping to the heavy downbeat of the rotors while being rocked in the cradle of a racing Black Hawk was her norm. Maybe the stability of the massive C-17 is what was throwing her off.

She didn't want to think that it might be his enigmatic smile that was costing her precious sleep. She'd expected him to be pissed at her trick—the other two spotters certainly had been—not smile.

JD Ramírez was a classic Delta soldier—nothing about him stood out, at least to the untrained eye. It was the SEALs and Rangers who tended to have the big guys. A Delta had strength and skills like the other teams, but mostly they possessed an irrationally extreme perseverance against all odds. None of that showed on the outside.

While not overly handsome, that smile had completely altered her view of him. After thirty days of hounding after her to outperform every operator around her, his smile—so clear in her rifle scope—had been beyond radiant. And not as if her success was his doing; she knew *that* type of arrogance all too well.

No. It was as if he was proud of her in the way her father had been the day she'd joined up to defend their new country.

Cindy would be damned if she was going to get all sniffly. That wasn't in a Delta's personality matrix, but she still couldn't shake that smile. It was a long time before the engine roar anesthetic kicked in even enough to doze.

6
___

Turning his back on where Cindy Chavez lay beside him during the flight didn't help matters in the slightest. JD couldn't believe what he'd seen as she'd crawled out of that hawthorn. Bloody from a hundred thorn scratches— and a smile as big as the sun in the Kansas sky.

He remembered the first day he'd seen her. He'd been the lead range instructor at the shooting test during Operator Selection. A hundred and twenty applicants were down to fifteen before they reached him. His goal was to make sure that every one of the fifteen was also a top marksman. By this point in the selection, a missed target wasn't a black mark, instead it was an opportunity for instruction—right up until too many misses knocked the hopeful back for retraining.

You're not reading the heat shimmer correctly.

Don't hesitate before a heartbeat, instead plan for it. At a thousand meters, the surge of blood driven into muscle by a heartbeat could shift a shooter's aim by several meters.

Of the twelve who made it through the shooting test, there was one he never had to give a correction to, because she never missed. He'd placed her last on the second day of shooting, by which time the wind was kicking hard and gusty over the blazing pasture of the Range 37 stalking range. Undeterred, she'd finished the test with only two misses—an incredible achievement he was only able to match, not beat.

"How the hell did you do that, Cindy?" Without even thinking, he'd rolled over on the steel decking to face her. She was so close and so goddamn beautiful that he couldn't find the air to explain what he was asking about. He wasn't even sure himself anymore. They were close enough that, despite the dim red nightlight of the cargo bay, he could see every eyelash as her eyes fluttered open.

The Globemaster was transporting a pair of Black Hawks and a half dozen pallets of supplies to Colombia for the never-ending drug war. The crews and equipment crammed the eighty-by-eighteen foot bay solidly. Their vehicle—a totally incongruous Dodge Viper sports car that he couldn't wait to drive—rested on the last pallet in the line. The two of them lay on the C-17's sloped rear ramp close beside it. They'd be getting off much sooner than everyone else aboard.

She blinked at him in surprise.

"You actually talking to me, Master Sergeant?"

"Might be," not that he'd admit to it. And now he was close enough to smell her. The odors of the sniper exercise had survived her shower, but there was another, indefinable scent that almost had him reaching for her.

She smelled of wilderness, adventure, and a warm fire on a cold winter night.

"Will wonders never cease," she muttered, little louder than the engine roar. "How did I do what? Climb a tree with no one noticing?"

"You did that by ignoring the rules, which is one of the reasons you're on this mission. By the way, how close were you before you did that?"

"I was inside the shoot line for twenty minutes before Grizzly shot, but once I crawled there it seemed too simple."

"Too simple," he grunted out. The stalking test was one of the hardest challenges there was for a sniper, and she'd shown a level of confidence exceptional for even a Delta by not just taking her victory.

She nodded.

"Where did you learn such patience?" He'd meant to ask where she'd learned to shoot. Her eyes skittered aside strangely at his new question. "Don't lie now. You already cheated on the test this morning. One sin per day should be enough."

Her eyes slowly returned to focus on him. Made even darker by the Globemaster's dim lighting, they seemed to reveal more of her than they ever had before. "Are you sure?"

"Am I sure of what?"

"That one sin per day is enough."

He propped his head onto his fist, with his elbow placed on the steel deck so that he could look at her more clearly. Unsure of what she was referring to, he shrugged and hoped that she'd continue on her own. The engine roar seemed to build during her continued silence until it wrapped around them like a cocoon.

Now it was her turn to shrug before speaking. "What's the real reason you've been pushing at me so hard all month? It's not gender bias. I figured that one out on my own."

"I need you for this assignment. I need a top-performing woman."

"There's your one sin for the day. Now try again, without the half-lie."

"Some day you'll have to tell me how you did that."

She shrugged maybe yes, maybe no.

JD looked at her. Really looked. They lay closer together than he'd ever been to her. As her eyes were telling him nothing, he watched her lips for some hint of her thoughts. He could just lean in and—

Get himself tossed into lockup for sexual harassment.

"I'm pushing you away because..." Because he was an idiot. He should be doing anything he could to bring her close. Though much closer and they'd be in each other's arms.

Her gaze almost skittered aside again, but this time locked and held.

"You a hypnotist too?" he barely managed to whisper.

7

Cindy wished she had a US Army Field Manual on men. JD Ramírez had been pushing her away because... he was attracted to her?

"What kind of sense does that make?"

His eyes crossed for a moment as he puzzled at her question.

"You're attracted to me?"

"No," his voice was flat, almost harsh again.

"Then *what?*"

He reached out and brushed a finger along her cheek.

It sent a chill of surprise through her so strong that she couldn't suppress the shudder.

"It's nothing as mild as that," he whispered. Then he blinked hard as if suddenly coming awake.

"Shit!"

He sat up abruptly, leaving her lying on the sloped rear ramp trying to gather her thoughts that had just scattered to the horizon faster than the big jet's turbulent wake.

He didn't go far. JD yanked off his jacket and leaned back against the charcoal gray sports car's bumper and faced her with his knees pulled up and his elbows resting on them.

She sat up and looked at him. They were toe to toe. Beyond him she could see the 101st Airborne fliers and grunts and a couple squads of 75th Rangers. Some slept, some were joking around. There was a poker game going on in one of the helo's open cargo bays. They were all leaving the two Delta Force operators, their hot car, and their secret mission alone.

Her insides were far less orderly. Everything was tied up in knots. JD didn't hate her, which was news in itself. But he also wasn't attracted to her—it was "nothing as mild as that." What came after that was only too clear.

"You pushed me so hard so that...so that I wouldn't want to be around you?"

He nodded, then shrugged, then shook his head. But he wasn't looking up from his boots either.

"I'm a patient person, JD, but you'd better explain yourself because I suck at guessing games."

"Where did you get such patience?" He glanced up at her, looked away, appeared to realize what he was doing and finally faced her squarely.

"Change of subject."

"I asked first, and earlier."

"No way, José Domingo."

"That's not my name."

"What is it then?"

He shook his head.

She growled in frustration. "Enough shit, Jesús

Dominic or whatever your name is. Speak or I'll beat the crap out of you. Right here. Right now. Faster than even any of the 75th Rangers can save you."

His smile invited her to try and she was almost tempted. When she didn't, he studied the ceiling of the Globemaster's cargo bay for a long moment before responding.

"I've never met a woman like you, Cindy Sue," this time it was a friendly tease rather than derision.

So she only kicked his calf hard enough to make him flinch. He held up a hand to show that he'd finally gotten the message.

"The way you shoot. The way you look. Both sexy as hell." He made a point of scanning down her body.

They were both dressed in para-military-civilian-on-holiday mode: well-worn boots, cargo pants with a few too many pockets, black t-shirts, and jeans jackets. She ignored his full-body scan, because she was doing the same. Out of his jacket and frustrated past speech, he looked beyond amazing.

"But it's the way you think that truly knocks me back. I've read your entire record, probably know it better than you do I've read it so many times. You don't just think outside the box—you don't even see it. I should have known you'd hunt me from behind," he laughed with delight.

It should be irritating, but she loved the sound of his laugh.

Then he sobered abruptly. "Look. I never meant to say any of this. If you want out, we'll scrub this mission and I'll find another way in."

A sleek, late-model Dodge Viper sports car. Two Deltas posing as an adventure-seeking paramilitary couple who both looked Latino and were fluent enough in Mexican-accented Spanish to sound local. Pretending to be out of work and looking for fun in the heart of Mexico's drug country.

They were on a kingpin hunt.

Most of the cartels were personality cults run by one or two charismatic individuals. Taking out El Chapo had broken the chokehold of the Sinaloa Cartel. But others had risen in their place to take advantage of the sudden weakness. Time to infiltrate and take down some more kingpins.

It was a fantastic chance for an important and exciting assignment.

And with JD Ramírez, the best soldier she'd never served with. But what if he was more than that?

Cindy liked the way that sounded.

She liked it a lot.

"No. I'll stay." But she couldn't make it too easy on him, or his ego might get out of hand. "I think this mission sounds interesting. I like a challenge."

8

JD still couldn't get a read on what Cindy was thinking. She was not a woman who wore her thoughts on her sleeve. Or on those beautiful lips.

Her smile had either said that's all she thought the op was, an interesting challenge. Or was it some sort of double entendre about himself. He just couldn't tell. He could hope, but he couldn't tell.

Once they were seated side-by-side in the Viper—hot lady in hot car inside a combat aircraft, damn but he was doing *something* right—he reached into the miniscule glove compartment. The car's cockpit was so tight, he was practically in her lap to do so. He still didn't know if that was welcome or not, so he pulled back as fast as he could.

"Here's your ID." He handed her a battered set of Mexican papers.

She riffled them open, "Gloria Chavez."

"I thought it would be easy for you to remember to respond to because you're so freaking glorious." And he really needed to remember when to shut up.

Cindy— No! Gloria, for the duration of this mission, held the papers to her chest as if they were somehow special.

Before he could ask what she was thinking—not a chance she would tell him but he wanted to ask anyway —the loadmaster tapped on the hood of the car. Then he raised a hand as if pulling up the parking brake.

JD made sure it was raised, then gave a thumbs up.

The loadmaster began knocking loose the tie-down chains on each tire.

"What's your name?"

"I'm Juan David Ramírez on my papers."

"What's your real name?"

The loadmaster lowered the C-17 Globemaster's rear ramp. It opened to reveal the dark of night and a remote stretch of a gravel road deep in the Sonoran Province south of Nogales.

He tried to find some way to not answer the question, but couldn't find one.

He stomped down on the brake and started the car's engine. It thrummed to life. He could feel the vibration, but the redoubled roar from the jet and the open cargo bay door completely drowned the sound out.

"Jimmy Dean."

"Like the sausage?"

He sighed, "*Exactly* like the sausage. My parents wanted an American sounding name and didn't know much English when I was conceived."

Her laugh sparkled to life. She reached out a hand and rested it on his arm as if to steady herself. It was the first time they'd ever touched, other than that one stolen brush of his finger down her cheek—the softness of her skin had almost undone him there and then. She'd become a thousand times more real in that moment.

Now, with her fingers wrapped lightly around his bare forearm, energy jolted through him like lightning.

"You asked how I was so patient?" The laugh still bubbled in her voice.

"Yes?" JD responded cautiously. Now he wasn't so sure he wanted to hear her answer.

The loadmaster flashed ten fingers twice. Twenty seconds.

JD slipped the car into third gear, but kept his foot on the clutch. He hit the headlights, and the outside world leaped to visibility. Beyond the open hatch and a dozen meters below, a two-lane unpaved road raced away from them. Off to the side, lay nothing but dirt and scrub brush.

"You kept me at a distance by chapping my ass."

Cin—Gloria didn't make it a question, so he didn't do more than nod.

The loadmaster held up ten fingers. Ten seconds to go. They flew five meters above the road.

"I kept you at a distance with my patience. I made myself learn it so that I wouldn't just fall into your arms."

He risked glancing over at her. "Since when?"

Her smile was glowing. The same smile she'd worn after climbing down out of that hawthorn tree with her face all bloodied. The same smile she'd first shown him after acing the marksmanship test all the way back in Delta Selection.

"Since the first time I met you, Master Sergeant JD

Ramírez. I pushed like I never had before—to get you to notice me."

"It worked. Mary Mother of God but it worked."

The loadmaster thumped on the hood and flashed three fingers at him.

Cindy locked her fingers around his arm.

The surge of joy passed into her as he dumped the brake and the car began to roll down the ramp.

The Dodge Viper gathered speed just as the steel ramp struck sparks and whirled a cloud of dust from the graveled surface.

Cindy braced for the jolt of the combat drop.

Her heart was racing, but not with the adrenaline of the tires hitting the roadway at just over a hundred miles an hour. Nor was it the deep throaty roar of the C-17 battling back aloft the instant they were unloaded to continue its journey south. The American military plane had never actually touched wheels in Mexico.

Glorious? He saw her as glorious.

He was right. It had worked. She was attracted, no, drawn to him like no one else in her life. That he felt the same was indeed a fantastic gift.

JD dropped the car into gear and, without slacking off the speed one bit, they raced off into the night. She could feel his muscles as he found the right gear for swooping over the rough road. She kept her hand on his arm because that's where it belonged.

Juan David and Gloria.

Maybe they'd just choose their names permanently, as they'd chosen their careers in Delta.

Maybe, after months of playing at being a couple, she'd choose Gloria Ramírez.

As they raced through the night toward a new adventure, she knew there was no doubt about it.

When she leaned over to kiss him on the cheek, he fishtailed hard on the gravel for a moment. Then he grinned over at her and punched it up another gear.

Together they flew down the road.

HER HEART AND THE 'FRIEND' COMMAND

Military War Dog handler Liza Minot finally lands her big chance. A Delta Force mission requires her and Sergey's specialty—tracking explosives.

When assigned to Master Sergeant Garret Conway's squad, her past confronts her. Back in high school days, he ran over her first dog. Rex's old age and failing health made it either a cruelty or a mercy—she still can't decide which. However, Conway the boy and Conway the man are two vastly different problems.

Only with her war dog's help can they both break free of their past to track down Her Heart and the "Friend" Command.

INTRODUCTION

This story arrived at a curious time in my writing career.

I had only written one other dog story before this one, *Reaching Out at Henderson's Ranch* (HR #2), a full year earlier.

But a fan who helps train MWDs convinced me that the Henderson's Ranch series needed more dogs in it. So I'd been madly researching MWDs (Military War Dogs). Little did I know at that time that it would become the defining core of the Henderson's Ranch series as well as the (then) barely conceived White House Protection Force series.

This story was a complete experiment.

Could I write an MWD into the center of the story *and* the center of the romance?

I could go on for pages about these dogs because they're simply that amazing. So I'll restrain myself, mostly. I will say that there are several quite distinct training regimens for dogs, and there's surprisingly little overlap:

- Drug sniffer
- Human tracker – so sensitive that they can find humans on the run, trapped under the rubble of a collapsed building (or an avalanche), or even buried underground like a mass grave
- Pure attack/protection – guard dogs
- Bomb sniffer – who can also perform attacks

You can actually train a dog to find almost anything, their nose is on the order of two hundred times more sensitive than a human's, but these are the main ones.

Anyway, so I knew my key character was Sergey the dog.

But the setting became a remarkably interesting challenge of its own.

Afghanistan is a completely landlocked country. To the north lie three of the 'stans and a tiny, very mountainous border with China. To the west lies Iran. And to the south and east lies Pakistan.

This meant that a hundred percent of supplies for the War in Afghanistan either had to be airlifted (incredibly expensive) or driven overland from Karachi, Pakistan.

There are only two real road crossings along the thousand-mile border. Which means that not only US military supplies but also the supplies for ISIS and the Taliban had to flow over those same border crossings.

To say that this makes an incredible mess is an understatement.

But I discovered another very curious feature to these crossings. Just on the Afghanistan side of the southern crossing, there are massive warehouses. U-Store would love to have that franchise.

Why?

Because so many of the Afghan refugees cross here. But only at the border do the people wealthy enough to have belongings discover that, for the most part, they can't take them across.

So, huge volumes of personal goods are left in these warehouses on the chance that the owners can ever return to collect them.

And there I had my setting, one ideal for the skills of a dog like Sergey.

1

———

"Today's the day, Sergey."

He watched her as she lashed on her fatigues, boots, vest, and helmet. His eyes tracked every motion as she stood over her pack in the safehouse bedroom. A grand word for a faded concrete cube, peeling whitewash, and a steel cot that might have once been comfortable, but certainly wasn't anymore. A tiny window let in the last of the day's red light and the occasional whirl of the bitter dust that southern Afghanistan used for soil.

"You'd make me feel crazy self-conscious, Sergey, if you weren't a dog." Her fifty-five pound Malinois war dog popped to his feet as she knelt beside him to strap on his own Kevlar vest. Normally he'd be kenneled rather than curled up at the foot of her bunk but, since the US military had sent her to a forward operating base in Afghanistan hell, such amenities were non-existent. She far preferred having her big furry boy asleep at her feet. They both did.

"Of course, Delta Force never is anywhere normal, are

we?" She slipped the vest over his head and smoothed it down his back. Flipping the chest strap between his front legs, she buckled it into the belly of the harness. One more strap farther back and he was fully geared up. She double-checked the feed from the flip-up camera on his back and tested the infrared nightlight. Both showed up clearly on her wrist screen and her night-vision goggles. All set for a little nightwork. The small window filled with the last red of the sunset meant they'd be on the move soon.

Delta Force. We. That was such a cool sound. She'd made it. Sideways, but she'd made it into the most elite fighting force anyway. Even Delta needed MWDs—military war dogs, though she preferred multi-pawed wagging detectors—and dogs for Special Operations needed their Spec Ops handlers. Dogs for the regular forces could transfer from one handler to the next, but it took a very special person to manage a dog trained to Delta standards.

"You are so handsome in your vest, aren't you?" She rubbed his ears then brushed her hands down his legs, an automatic gesture in which she checked for everything from burrs in the fur to the condition of underlying muscle and bone.

"Where do I sign up for such treatment, Minnow?"

She sighed. Of course no world was perfect.

Elizabeth Minot—the nickname had been inevitable despite her family pronouncing it My-not—didn't bother to look up at the male voice; didn't need to turn to know what he looked like.

Garret Conway would have shoved aside the aging

drape that served as the room's door with a military disregard for gender. He'd be slouching against one of the jambs, arms crossed over his chest as he glared down at the two of them with his dark brown eyes. He wasn't much taller than she was, Delta selection didn't favor tall and strong, but rather the driven and powerful. Dark hair worn long, a trim beard that eased the hard lines of his face.

So instead, she continued talking to Sergey as she finished checking him over. Pads of his paws...tail. As always, she tweaked the tip for good luck which earned her a doggie smile. All good.

"Maybe if the nasty sergeant promised to love me for a Kong dog toy and a crunchy biscuit, I'd deign to talk to him." Like she'd give the arrogant bastard the time of day. He'd been an utter twit of a boy back in the blue-collar core of Baltimore—the Dundalk neighborhood being the only thing they had in common. And just because he'd grown up into a seriously handsome soldier didn't make him any less of an SOB. She knew his dark side all too well and it was just one of the trials that the Powers That Be had placed across her path, landing her on *his* team after she'd rarely thought of him for a decade.

The fates were off at a bar crawl somewhere laughing their asses off for saddling her with him as the squad leader of her first-ever deployment with Delta. It had been a rude shock when she'd arrived this morning.

Master Sergeant Garret Conway was going to be a problem.

"Do you think he'd like a dog toy?" She asked Sergey.

To make her point, Liza bounced Sergey's Kong toy on the wooden floor of the safehouse they were squatting in.

The hard rubber, shaped like a five-inch marshmallow man, ricocheted in an unexpected direction, sending Sergey pouncing, missing, and pouncing again as his attack sent it off in another direction. A frantic scuffle ensued—which included a brief strike beneath the sad excuse for a bunk—before Sergey sat back, the triumphant winner of the tussle. He smiled up at her proudly with the adoration clear in his eyes. He gave her the Kong and she traded it for a doggie treat from her pouch.

The Kong and treat were why MWDs worked so hard. They didn't care about explosives. They just knew that when they sniffed out the explosives, they got the toy then the treat.

She fished out another treat and held it out to the squad's leader—that's how she'd think of him. Not friend —never was. Not even acquaintance from Baltimore. He'd just be Master Sergeant Conway, her Delta Force squad leader.

"Want one?" Though why she was teasing him, she didn't know.

Garret managed to take the small treat without touching her fingers. He eyed her as he bounced it in his palm. He'd been the lean and dangerous kid in high school and she could still see it in his narrowed eyes though he'd certainly filled out since then. Nobody had messed with Garret—nobody dared. He'd always had a circle of wannabes, but he hadn't needed them. It was more as if he was a one-man center of dark power and the others had merely been drawn like night moths. No matter where she went in the school, it had always seemed that he was there in the background watching. He missed nothing.

Occasionally, if she'd wanted to track someone down, she'd ask him. That was about the only time they ever spoke, but he always knew. She knew almost nothing about him. His dad was a stevedore down at the port—the kind who drank too much when he got home. Her dad was a machinist who didn't. It bothered her that she couldn't remember more about him.

Garret had always had a hot girl under his arm at every school dance or block party. He'd never been picky on the last count: athlete, cheerleader, from another school (a big social crime that only he could get away with), slut... Never mattered as long as she was built. Liza once again blessed her lean figure that had served her so well in track and field, and in the Army. Surviving her three brothers had developed her strength early and she'd never let that advantage go.

When her dad had slipped a German Shepard pup under the tree for her fifth Christmas, she'd found her calling. The two of them had played and run together until a car had killed him when she was seventeen. By then he was slow, mostly deaf, and blind in one eye.

She'd been walking him home from the vet who had given the worst pronouncement of all—cancer, with only days to live. She often wondered if Rex had known what he was doing when he'd stepped off the curb before she released him. It had been instantaneous, merciful, and utterly horrifying. When she'd looked up from Rex's suddenly lax form into Garret Conway's eyes, she didn't know whether to thank him or try to kill him.

Liza still didn't.

Garret continued to watch her as he fooled with the treat. Then—with no more words than he'd offered on that horrible day while he'd put Rex in her lap in the back seat and driven her back to the vet to arrange for cremation—he held the treat out for Sergey.

Sergey's sharp snarl had him jerking his hand back.

"What the hell?"

"I haven't told him that you're a friend. He's very careful."

"So tell him, Minnow." Half the high school had gone to "Little Fish." At least he'd never done that.

Tell Sergey that Garret was a friend? Not in a thousand years. But the dog only knew the one word. She had no way to explain "asshole from my past but don't attack him" to a dog. There was *friend* and there was *attack*.

Finally, she simply said, "Down."

Sergey lay down immediately, but continued glaring at Garret. *Good dog.*

2

GARRET DIDN'T KNOW WHICH OF THE TWO LOOKED MORE dangerous: the tall slip of a blonde or her damn dog. It was clear that neither was glad to see him.

Of all the possible soldiers command could have sent his way, why did it have to be her? Had someone seen the shared high school in their past and decided they were doing him a favor? No. They'd looked at skills and decided she was the best fit for the job based on skills and availability—meaning she'd already been in the dustbowl rather than having to be shipped in from the States.

He didn't doubt that for a second. She'd always been one of those overachiever types. A top student and the school's star decathlete. After watching her win seven of ten events in a decathlon, easily winning the overall event freshman year, he'd tried out for the team. That's when he'd discovered what an amazing athlete she truly was. The coach had kicked him loose after three events: not the first cut, but almost. Thank god she hadn't been around that day to see his humiliation.

The next year, he'd made it through all of the events before being cut. He'd finally made the team the year she went All-State—the football team. He was fast and knew how to take a hit—but it wasn't enough to shine among the guys who'd caught their first pass as they were leaving the womb. He'd graduated second string and hadn't liked it.

Minnow was the gold standard of women. It sucked that he'd never been able to speak to her. The beautiful, popular, star athlete shone with a brightness that made his life feel even darker and dirtier than it was.

He tossed the dog treat down in front of the Malinois. Sergey didn't even track it to the floor—his attention remained riveted on Garret's face, and not in a good way. His muscles remained bunched and ready for action.

"We've got some chow in the other room," he said to Minnow. "Briefing in ten. Out the door in twenty." Then he turned his back on them and walked back to join the rest of the team.

"It's okay," he heard her speak softly to the dog.

There was a sharp snap of jaws that took all of Garret's training not to react to. Then he heard the quick crunch as Sergey ate the treat he must have snapped up.

The hut's other room was just as disgusting as the sole bedroom he'd given Minnow and her dog. Their safehouse was little more than the smallest of three huts inside a massive ring of HESCO barriers and piles of sandbags. A dozen years of occupancy by a rotating stream of NATO forces hadn't been kind to it. A small firepit, a table covered in his team's gear, wooden pegs driven into cracks in the concrete from which their rifles dangled on their straps. Regular forces were standing security outside, so at least they didn't have to think about that. The other four Unit operators were too quiet and had clearly heard everything.

"Mutt and Jeff," Maxwell and Jaffe, the nickname inevitable as they were two jokers like a comedy routine, ping-ponging remarks back and forth. They could go all day if he let them. One tall and at least a little thoughtful, the other short and quick-witted. They were also both crack shots.

"Both of you load up long."

No need to tell them twice. They opened hard-shell cases and began assembling their preferred sniper rifles. Predictably Mutt favored an old-school Accuracy International AWM and Jeff ran with a hot-rod Remington M2010 that he'd hand-modified—only a true sniper tinkered with a ten thousand dollar rifle. Both were barreled for the .300 Win Mag cartridges, so that they could swap ammo if needed.

"BB," Burton and Baxter on the other hand, could be addressed interchangeably. As different and distinct as Mutt and Jeff were, the BB boys weren't. Both explosive and electronic techs, they were generally quiet but had a habit of finishing each other's sentences. No sign of a sense of humor, it was just something they did. One from Oregon, the other from Idaho and despite three years together he wasn't sure which one. They'd both kicked their pasts to the curb, which sounded good to him—as if he couldn't feel the past and her dog watching him through the doorway at his back.

It still felt strange to be in charge of the team. Chris had just recently opted out after his wife Azadah came down with an incurable condition, becoming mother of his first child. Since when did hard-core Delta operators turn all mushy? The answer: since he'd fallen in love with an Afghan refugee during the team's three-month deployment in Lashkar Gah and taken her home. Just because she'd helped them take down some of the top "most wanted" in southern Afghanistan was no reason to fall in love with her. At least not that he could see.

What had been crazy was that none of them had noticed her while she'd been working as their cook and charwoman—except Chris. Yet when Garret had seen her at the wedding in upstate New York, she was so stunning it was hard to believe. High-born, fallen on hard times during all of the wars, fluent in several languages (including a soft English), she had somehow shifted from being invisible to being impossible to look away from. The woman had glowed and Chris, the lucky asshole, had never looked so happy in the six years he and Garret had served together.

But Garret wasn't going to have any of that. He'd finally found himself in The Unit, as Delta called them themselves. No way was he leaving except if they carried him out and *that* was something no operator really thought about.

It felt even stranger being in charge with Liza aboard.

He couldn't imagine that Minnow would be any less than an amazing asset—he just wasn't sure how he was going to survive it.

3

———

THERE HADN'T BEEN TIME TO REALLY MEET THE OTHERS when she'd slipped into Wesh, Afghanistan along with the pre-dawn light. The Unit had been returning from a long patrol and had crashed into their bedrolls. Even less talkative than normal for Unit operators; which was saying something. They'd obviously been pushing hard.

Unsure what to do or how to behave—and totally unnerved at finding Garret Conway in command—Liza had taken his gesture toward the back room as banishment and hunkered down. In the middle of the night she'd decided that there was no way he'd get the best of her and ruin her first chance with The Unit.

So, she entered the main room as confidently as she could.

Sergey was her envoy. She kept him on a tight lead, which was completely for show as she could command him much more accurately and quickly with gestures and voice commands.

She greeted each one the same way, "If you'd hold out

your hand for Sergey to get your scent." As each one did, she'd clearly say, "Friend." Each time Sergey would look up at her to make sure, then take a sniff and accept a pat on the head.

"Don't know what your problem is, Conway," tall-and-lean Mutt tickled Sergey's ears. "Looks like a sweetheart to me."

"Just a big old mushball, aren't you?" Jeff, Mutt's short-and-solid sidekick, gave her dog a neck rub.

"I don't know..." Baxter was more interested in checking out the vest with light and camera than the animal wearing it.

"...looks ready for a Spec Ops mission to me," Burton finished. Both were middle-build and Nordic blond. It would be hard not to get them mixed up except that Burton paid some attention to Sergey before checking out the dog's military vest himself. He looked to Sergey rather than her for permission before he reached out to toy with the camera—a gesture Liza appreciated.

The infrared and daylight camera was center-mounted on his back with a flip mount so that it could fold forward or back in case Sergey needed to squeeze in or out of a small space. It also had an infrared light to really illuminate the darkness when needed. A Lexan faceplate protected the lens. The antenna mounted close beside it was a flexible whip rather than a knockdown.

Then they both inspected the feed to the screen on Liza's wrist.

"Very cool!" Baxter noted.

"Thanks!" Burton rubbed Sergey's head in appreciation for his patience.

She had the feeling that she was invisible to the men, as she often did when Sergey was beside her. No complaints from her. Let them focus on the dog, she didn't need their praise, only his.

Then she turned to Garret...no, Conway. Everyone else called him Conway and so would she. Once more he slouched against a wall, sporking his way through an MRE—Meal-Ready-to-Eat—straight out of the bag. Shredded BBQ Beef, with black beans and notoriously soggy tortillas, for breakfast.

She stopped Sergey two steps from Conway. Sergey didn't strain on the leash, but she could feel his tension vibrating up its length. Or maybe her tension vibrating down it.

The dog always knows what the trainer feels, she repeated her trainer's prime axiom. *Always. So only feel what you want the dog to feel.*

Liza took a deep breath to calm herself.

"Friend," she managed. Though it was harder than she'd expected—and she hadn't thought it would be easy.

Sergey and Conway both looked at her in surprise. Here was one man who saw her clearly behind the dog. He lowered his hand for Sergey to smell, but didn't look away from her.

She could feel her dog still looking at her in question.

"It's okay," she repeated, though she wasn't sure for whose benefit.

4

Last night's patrol—and the five nights before that —had narrowed down their mission. Narrowed it down enough for Garret to know they'd need all the help they could get, specifically from a MWD. He'd sent the request up the chain of command and they'd sent back down Sergey and Minnow.

Time to just live with it. Just this one assignment, then she'd be gone back into the vast world of US Army Human Resources Command and wash up on someone else's shore. That knowledge, like so much in the military, was both a relief and a knife to the gut.

He unrolled the map of Wesh, Afghanistan, and the near edge of Chaman, Pakistan, separated by the towering, dual-arched Friendship Gate.

"The Durand Line, the border between Afghanistan and Pakistan, is over two thousand kilometers long from Iran up to India. It is generally named as the most dangerous border in the world—which if you've done time in Korea you know is saying something. The two countries have been fighting over it ever since the line was first drawn in 1893 by the Brits and the Afghan Amir. Oddly, Pakistan is fine with the line, it's the Afghanis who say they'll never accept the border."

"Whoever would want this stretch of desert is welcome to it."

"Pashtuns, dude." Mutt and Jeff were at it again. "The Pashtun tribes cover thousands of square kilometers on both sides."

"Then why are they killing each other if they're all Pashtuns?"

"Not our business," Garret cut them off. Because there were a hundred layers of answers to that question: some historical, some religious, some about power, and none of it good for the locals.

He could feel Minnow assessing their group dynamics. It made him see himself and all his flaws as a commander as if seeing himself through stranger's eyes. Too rough? Or just holding the team's focus? He couldn't think how to change the patterns even if he understood what they were. Chris had always made it look so easy. How was he supposed to know that leadership was such a pain in the ass.

"Our business is that Wesh-Chaman is the only crossing for hundreds of kilometers in both directions. All through the Afghan War—"

"Which one?"

And again it spun out of his control before he even—

"The one that started with Alexander the Great. That was like three hundred AD or something."

"Three-thirty BC, dude, learn your history. And no,

he's talking about the one that started in 1978 with the Communist Insurrection and hasn't stopped since. Next came the Soviets, the communist collapse, the Taliban, and then us. No wonder this place is a disaster area. Did you know—"

"Shut up, Jeff," Garret shut them down harder this time. "I'm talking about the US War in Afghanistan and you assholes know it so give me a goddamn break. This Wesh-Chaman crossing has been our major supply route since Day One for all of southern Afghanistan. Still is, since we haven't really left, and it's coming apart, again. Tonight we're going to put some of it back together, again."

"Good. I was getting bored. How about you, Sergey?" Mutt rubbed the dog's neck where he lay between Mutt and Liza. Sergey just scowled up at him, Garret-radar on red alert. The dog wasn't having anything to do with the "friend" instruction no matter what Minnow commanded.

Garret continued. "They sent in a reinforced platoon of over sixty regular Army, and they found squat. Now it's Delta's turn."

The five of them, a woman, and her dog.

"The US has had constant problems with the Paki gunrunners supplying the Afghanis. In turn, the Pakis have been getting nailed by the Afghani militants who think shelling civilians across the border during a census-taking makes some kind of sense. Just last week they blew up another pair of fuel tanker semi-trucks. Not like the sixteen they got at once back in 2009, but—"

"Can you imagine what..." Baxter joined in for the first time.

"...two hundred thousand gallons was like..." Burton was on it.

"...all at once?" Baxter sighed for having missed such a spectacle.

"Ka-boom!" they said together and both sighed again. They were both explosives techs, so he let them have their moment.

"I'm lead," Garret told them. "BB, you're both hot on my tail. Mutt and Jeff, you alternate sniper overwatch and watching the back doors."

"Where do you want us?" Liza had her hand dug into the dog's fur. He could see that her knuckles were white no matter how calm her voice was.

"You, Minnow, are glued to my hip."

And wasn't that going to be fun.

5

The buildings of Wesh were pitch black—invisible except as dark notches out of the stars. Without her night-vision goggles she couldn't have made it ten steps. No street lights and what electricity the town did have was apparently on the fritz per usual in small Afghan towns. A few windows were lit by the flickering of oil lamps, a very few. It was a town without air conditioning, and one that needed it desperately. She and Sergey had been tramping through Afghan hell for three months now and neither of them were any more used to the heat than the day they landed.

"What are we after?" Liza eased down the narrow street far closer to Garret Conway than she'd ever been to him in high school. Much to her surprise, she'd liked watching him with the men. Whatever else she might think of him, his men trusted him completely. This wasn't some cluster of sycophantic hallway teens; these were top Unit operators.

"Sergey's specialty," Garret kept his voice low. "There

is a constant stream of explosives moving in both directions here. Bombs for inbound NATO supply trucks headed into Kandahar and Lashkar Gah. And Taliban and other pissed-off Afghanis going into Pakistan to blow the crap out of shrines and the civilian populace. I don't care which side is holding it, I just want it gone. No matter which way it's headed, it comes through Wesh. We want the bombmakers and their middlemen."

Wesh was laid out differently than most Afghan towns she'd patrolled. Usually they were a rabbit warren of streets which had evolved for donkeys and pedestrians. But the old Silk Road had passed through here since the Romans began trading with the Chinese and probably before that. The town was sliced by the one wide main street that must date back thousands of years. Rather than being lined with haphazard two-story structures that were connected only by the chance of shared walls, the main road was lined to either side with long rows of stone one-story warehouses. Each warehouse was a great V with dozens of storefronts and storage bays facing inward—the open end of the V facing the trade road. They served the only passage between the countries for a long way around.

At the head of the first V, Garret stopped at the corner of the building where they were in deepest shadow.

BB were close behind them.

Jeff had peeled off to go down the back side of the building in case they flushed anyone out that way.

Conway tapped her shoulder then pointed across the street and up. With her night-vision goggles, she could just make out Mutt on top of the only two-story building for several hundred meters around. He then indicated for her to lead the way, pointing close along the line of closed shops.

She turned on the feed from Sergey's camera in one eye of her NVGs. For brightness, she selected a level that didn't distract her, but she could see as an overlay if she concentrated on it. Originally, it had been a vertiginous experience—disorienting dog-style motion fed into the human eye—but she'd learned to use and finally appreciate it. Wherever Sergey went, she could feel the connection between them until they functioned as one.

She knelt next to Sergey, gave him a good scratch, then whispered, "Seek." A hand gesture—that she knew he could see even if it was too dark for unaided human eyes—was all the direction he needed.

In that instant, he transformed. He would no longer react well to anyone trying to touch him, but neither would he be bothered by Garret Conway standing a foot away. He now had only one task in mind—sniffing out one of the thousand-plus explosives compounds he'd been trained to recognize.

Trusting her, he stepped around the corner and began working his way along the line of shops. She swung loose her FN-SCAR assault rifle, double-checked that the flash suppressor was in place and moved in behind him. Sergey trailed his nose along the base of battered wood and steel garage doors that shuttered each bay of the long building.

Fifty meters down, he skipped a narrow doorway, probably leading up a set a stairs to the roof. She snapped her fingers lightly, calling him back. He double-checked where she indicated, but showed no interest, so she waved him to continue.

After the third building with no "alert," she could feel the team's growing impatience.

But she knew she couldn't share that. Couldn't let Sergey know or he'd pick up on it, get distracted or hurry at the wrong moment.

She signaled him along the fourth building and followed in his footsteps.

6

———

GARRET DIDN'T KNOW WHETHER TO BE THRILLED OR worried. If his team had been searching on their own, they'd still be back at the first building, breaking into bay after bay of worthless garbage. Some of it would be household belongings, stored when refugees had been told they couldn't take them across the border—all held in the hopes of returning someday. Foodstuffs, manufacturing supplies, bicycle parts, the list was endless. The locks were feeble at best, easily picked. But each lock took time. Each inspection was visual and usually tedious.

But the dog went by each bay as fast as they could walk.

This was either fast...or useless. What if they'd walked by some major weapons cache?

He'd worked with military war dogs before, but always as point on a patrol, sniffing out buried IEDs. He'd never let a MWD guide the destination of an entire mission.

As they moved to the fifth warehouse, he couldn't help watching Minnow. She moved like her nickname: quick, smooth, hardly disturbing the air around her. In a land where standing still and just breathing could produce a rising cloud of brownout dust, she and her dog barely stirred the air as they slipped along.

Get her out of your head, Conway! Being distracted by anything on a mission was bad news. He thought that had been trained out of him, but apparently not.

Liza could distract a dead man already in his grave. That pleasant, can-do attitude she'd struck with the team this evening had been pitch perfect. She'd won all four guys over with her polite introduction and her ever-so-gentle but obviously dangerous-as-hell companion. He pitied the man who tried to touch her uninvited.

Minnow had also stood out because of how she looked. They'd all been in-country for a week and looked it. She'd arrived from wherever she'd been, looking fresh-showered and poster perfect. Her straight blonde hair swinging just along her fine jaw line. Her blue eyes wide and observant. Her smile easy—for everyone except him. And the way she acted with the dog was just too much.

Like the one that he'd murdered and never been able to apologize for, it was clear that she loved her dog and that the feeling was returned. Together they—

Sergey sat abruptly and Garret almost plowed into Minnow when she stopped as well.

The dog was looking up at her expectantly, his tongue lolling happily.

"What?" He was so close to her that he barely had to whisper. As close as lovers.

Shit! He'd just been in the field too long. Had to be to think such things.

Minnow made the throat-cutting signal with her hand meaning danger, then pointed emphatically at the closed door.

Oh! Pay dirt. Sitting was the dog's signal of a find.

She quickly guided Sergey forward, pointing at the ground. He sniffed the ground, but kept walking. No IEDs. Then she led him to the opposite edge of the door. Once more he sat abruptly.

Garret clicked his mic and whispered, "West side, bay seven."

Jeff was now on sniper overwatch and Mutt was on the ground out back. Mutt would position himself to deal with anyone trying to escape that way.

Burton came forward to pick the lock, but hesitated at the door. He swung his hand forward, the sign for point of entry. Then he made an non-standard gesture like twisting a doorknob. Like—

There was no lock for him to unlock. Garret checked the door edges again. No light leakage. It was a double, wooden door, with handles and a wear line where a chain and padlock had hung. The doors would swing out to either side.

In case it was booby-trapped, or a gunman waited in the dark, Garret yanked out a length of tactical line and tied it to one handle. Burton did the same to the other door. He had them switch sides, which confused Burton, but that was just tough. They each backed up holding the end of the line. Burton stood beside Baxter and, as he'd planned, Garret ended up between Minnow and the dog.

He held up three fingers...two...braced himself, then yanked open the doors.

A heavy sheet of black plastic hung just inside the doors, blocking all light.

"*Tsook?*" a voice asked "Who?" through the black plastic.

Garret held up a fist to freeze the team in place.

Someone pulled aside one edge of the plastic less than two feet from where Garret stood with his back against the now open door. The man was backlit by a kerosene or oil lamp and would be night blind. Like most Afghan men, he was thin, weather-beaten, and wore a thin black beard.

"*Tsook?*" he asked again.

Garret reached out, grabbed him by the throat, and dragged him out through the plastic. As the material flapped aside, he didn't see anyone else inside. He thumped the man in the solar plexus hard enough to make sure he wouldn't be crying out an alarm in the next few moments, then passed him back to the soldier behind him.

That would be Minnow! *Crap!* No choice. He handed the man off and hoped for the best.

He used his rifle barrel to brush aside the plastic as Baxter did the same on the other side. Two women squatted low over an entire array of armament. There were dozens of AK-47s and several rocket-propelled grenades. An old Toyota Land Cruiser SUV was stripped down, ready to be turned into a rolling bomb. Everything would be hidden inside door panels, fenders, and seats. The only thing they lacked was a pile of something that exploded to shove inside the exposed cavities.

In moments, Minnow had handed off her prisoner and had the two women bound. Dealing with another woman, the two Afghani women were surprised, but calm. If a man had done it, they'd fight and scream because no married woman was supposed to be touched by another man. Minnow hadn't missed a single trick. No matter how fresh she looked, she'd clearly spent plenty of time in-country.

He squatted down and began questioning the man, who just kept shaking his head in refusal.

That's when he noticed Minnow. She had Sergey playing his nice-doggie game. Garret never heard the word "friend" but neither was the Malinois poised to rend.

Unable to get anything from the man, he finally gagged him just as Minnow signaled Garret to the other corner.

BB made fast work of completely securing the area and clearing the weapons.

"Couldn't get shit out of him," Garret grumbled.

"The women are waiting," Minnow replied. "They aren't happy about it either, but he's brother to one and husband to the other so they have little choice."

"For what?"

"There's a shipment coming tonight," she waved toward the partially disassembled car. "A big load of explosives. Coming here. Not for a while, but it's coming."

Now *that* was good news.

He stopped BB before they could burn some thermite

and melt the weapons cache. Everything had to look normal. He deployed his team as well as he could, restoring the black-out plastic, closing the doors, as well as arranging a few other surprises. He roamed the room. All the tools of a car mechanic's shop were piled along one wall, but no spare parts—new or used. The man was a car-bomb producer. Pull in a car, receive a delivery of explosives and, presto chango, mass destruction in a marketplace.

The front had been cleared for the pending delivery. A stripped Land Cruiser SUV stood in the middle of the bay. The guy was good. He'd welded steel struts in place of the springs. It would make for a hard ride, but the suspension wouldn't sag—a common indicator of a car loaded down heavy with explosives. Near one back corner, past the stack of dismounted fenders and seats, stood the refuse pile—all the stripped-out metal, springs, fittings, even spare tires from prior car-bomb conversions. There was a small gap along the back wall for access to the rear door. He made sure it was secure. To the other side stood a massive, rusted-out truck's engine block. He stashed his prisoners behind that.

At the center of the back wall he was able to sit with a view of the whole bay. He dropped into place with his back against the wall to do what Delta did best—be patient and wait.

A low growl informed him that he should have landed somewhere other than close beside Minnow and her furry guardian.

7

———

"Shush!"

Sergey huffed grumpily then lay his head on her thigh, effectively pinning her in place. That blocked any excuse for getting away from Conway.

"How long until the shipment arrives?" Conway checked his watch for the twentieth time in the last ten minutes.

"I still don't know."

"Right. Sorry."

They sat in silence long enough for Sergey to finally relax with a sigh.

"Doesn't like me much."

"You never gave *me* a reason to," which Liza decided was just the truth. She never had, though she was definitely learning to respect the man he'd grown into.

"Murdering your dog. Guess not." Liza could hear the hard knot of pain and self-recrimination in Conway's voice.

"He was dead already."

Conway glared at the ceiling. He'd rested his HK416 rifle butt down between his legs and draped his hands over the protrusion of the foregrip handle. "You saying that you tossed a dead dog in front of my car for the fun of it? I saw him walking."

Liza could feel that awful day coming back over her. Rex had slowed down the few days prior. He'd been old, but still enjoying his play and his food, then suddenly he didn't anymore. It had been everything she could do to not weep after the diagnosis as she walked him home. "One last walk to say goodbye." They'd spend one last night together in her bed then she'd have to put him down in the morning. And then...

"He was a dead dog walking," her voice sounded like a croaking frog, but she held it together. She certainly wasn't going to lose it in front of Garret Conway of all people. Or on a mission. She distracted herself by telling him about the blindness, deafness, and finally cancer. And not just a little, but riddling his body. "Sometimes I think he stepped in front of your car on purpose, just to spare me having to hold his paw while they injected him."

Now Garret was looking down at her, "He was sick? I didn't know."

She could only nod and look down at her hand buried deep in Sergey's fur.

After a long silence—that she couldn't look up from —she could feel him turn to study the ceiling once more. "Well, ain't that some news. You never said."

"The shock, Garret. It was so big. You hit him less than five minutes after I staggered out of the vet's office. I wasn't ready to lose him. Not slowly, not fast. Dad gave him to me when I was five. I have almost no memories prior to him. Then he was gone. It was a blessing in disguise. But I sure wasn't ready to talk about it that day. And afterwards..." all she could do was shrug. "We never spoke much in school."

She heard a soft *thump,* then another, and looked up to see him banging the back of his head against the stone wall.

"What?"

"You and that dog changed my life."

"No we didn't." It was a ridiculous idea.

Then he looked over at her. The deep brown of his eyes so close that she couldn't look away. They'd been almost shoulder-to-shoulder, and now they were nearly nose-to-nose.

"Trust me," his voice went soft and low. "You and he absolutely did."

8

____

AND GARRET COULDN'T BELIEVE HE'D JUST CONFESSED such a thing. *Keep it professional.* Yeah, too late for that. He was a Unit operator, not a throwback, useless-shit of a self-absorbed testosterone-laden... But he still couldn't believe he'd told her.

And the apology that he'd rehearsed a thousand times in his head, but never found a way to say through the rest of senior year, he couldn't manage now either.

He wanted to look away, he *needed* to look away. But there she was, looking at him with those wide blue eyes the color of a summer sky and he couldn't move. He'd often hung out at the piers along the Patapsco River, waiting for his dad and watching that sky. She was like the only good part of home.

"How did *my* dog change *your* life?"

"Not just your dog."

Sergey looked up suddenly, inspecting her rather than him. Then Garret noticed her white-knuckled hand buried in his ruff.

"Um, you may want to ease up on your dog there."

At that, she finally looked away and he felt as if he'd been released from some sort of hypnosis ray. She eased her death grip and apologized to the dog. Sergey inspected him with curiosity, but no longer animosity.

Then Minnow looked back up at him and he was trapped again by the eyes that were windows right down into her.

"How is it you're still single, Minnow?" Not a question he had ever thought he'd be asking.

She shrugged. "Why?"

"You—" he stumbled to a halt. "I—" *really need to shut the hell up.* "You—" he tried again. "Shit!" he gave up trying and went back to beating his head against the stone wall. Why couldn't the terrorist bastards just show up already? He'd take 'em down. Maybe get a lead on some arms supplier. Interrupt and destroy a big weapons delivery. He knew how to do those. How to talk to Liza Minot was obviously beyond him.

"Garret, you can't just say something like that and not explain it. How did my poor old dog change *your* life?"

Well, at least she was back to that topic. He had some chance of explaining that without screwing up.

"Because I could never run like you." Or perhaps he couldn't help screwing up around her. Giving up, he explained himself.

9

Liza could only watch Garret with amazement.

He explained his failed attempts to make the track-and-field team to get her attention. *Her* attention. She was a nobody, just a better-than-average student who had learned how to run and throw so that she could keep up with her older brothers. She been outfielder at home softball games by seven and pitcher by nine. Though after several "slobber ball" complaints, she'd had to teach Rex that if he wanted to sit on the mound with her, he wasn't allowed to chase softballs. Tennis balls, of course, were fair game. He was a major disruption when neighborhood games of stick ball had spilled out onto the hot summer streets.

"Your dog..."

Liza finally realized that Garret didn't even know Rex's name, so she told him.

"Thanks. Killing Rex made me give up on you. No way you were ever going to talk to the guy who murdered your dog."

"But it wasn't—"

"So you tell me now. I'm still not so sure. Anyway. I knew what I had to do. Even just to live with myself, I was going to have to get truly good at something."

"And you chose the toughest team in the entire military."

He nodded, "And I chose the toughest team in the entire military. Made it too."

She could hear the pride in his voice. Except he was a guy, so it was more like self-satisfaction. Now that he'd made it, *of course* he'd made it. As if any past doubts (and past failings) had been erased by his actual success.

And maybe they had.

"You're not the Garret Conway I knew in school."

"I'm hoping that's a good thing."

She didn't know how to answer, because she wasn't sure what the question was any more. He'd held some kind of a ludicrous torch for her, which had driven him into Delta. Yet, at the same time, he'd given up that torch, and thrown himself completely into becoming a truly superior soldier.

Somehow she and Rex had changed a man's life. And knowing that brought back all the grief she had shut down so hard all those years ago. She missed Rex all over again like a hole in her heart. Yet his final act had been to change a man's life for the better. And again she wondered if it had been conscious. Or some weird doggie sense of what was needed? It would be just too unlikely if it was merely coincidence.

Her head was whirling and she wondered if she was

going to lose the Maple Pork Sausage Patty with Pepper and Onions MRE that had been her breakfast hours ago.

"I'm going to go and check on things," Garret leveraged himself to his feet. But before he stepped away, he rested his hand on her shoulder for just a moment. "It's good to see you, Minnow." Then he was across the room checking nothing in particular that she could see.

THEY CAME AT MOONSET. THE DARKEST PART OF THE Afghan night.

Mutt and Jeff had a brief debate over which of them heard the vehicles first. The trucks were coming from the Afghanistan side, so the targets must be the Pakis—this time. Did this bombmaker service both sides? Probably not. He struck Garret as more the fanatic type.

Three Toyota pickups. Most of the traffic to the Friendship Gate was by foot, bicycle, and burro-drawn carts. The motorized traffic was almost entirely massive trucks. There were the NATO and US supply trucks carrying exactly the labeled load limit. These were accompanied by heavily armed patrols to deter anyone attaching an explosive charge to them. The other trucks were just as big, but loaded ludicrously beyond anything the rigs had ever been designed for. Loose hay, bags of grain or rice, stacks upon stacks of bricks, anything—all piled so high that it was a miracle the trucks didn't tip over every time they hit a pothole. These were driven with reckless abandon and had been a staple of the region since forever.

Small Toyotas were good utility trucks, but they were fantastic field vehicles for roving military. Tough, reliable, four-wheel drive, and able to carry a heavy load. Not armored, but cheap and plentiful.

Mutt and Jeff were both on rooftops now. They reported that two of the three were loaded to past the limits beneath heavy tarps. It was the middle vehicle that was worrisome. Someone had mounted a DShK Russian heavy machine gun on its bed. Its round could punch through an inch of armor. If that's what they had in the open, it meant the men in the cabs would have plenty of automatic weapons.

He yanked the Afghani to his feet and pulled his gag.

"You will say the code words, and you will say them properly."

When the man started to protest, Garret yanked his sidearm and rammed the barrel up under the man's jaw.

"*Pohidal?*"

He decided to take the man's wide eyes as a yes that he "understood."

Until Minnow called out to him, "The woman said that her husband is very stubborn."

"Shit!" He didn't have time for this. Garret swung his sidearm aside, then smashed it back against the man's temple. He dropped like a brick.

Minnow helped him drag the man back into a safe spot where the other two women were tied behind the truck engine block.

BB were front and back on the roof of this long arm of

the warehouse's V-shape, ready to fire from above or drop down if needed.

His snipers were on opposing rooftops for maximum coverage—one across the main street, the other looking down from the next block back.

That left him, Minnow, and her dog in the equipment bay itself. Bad planning, but his need to keep her close had gotten them here and it was too late to change their plan. Especially as his goal was to keep some of the bad guys alive long enough to get more information about the supply chain.

He crossed to where she was watching the back door from the same protected corner that held their three hostages.

"You keep low and you stay alive, hear?"

She nodded then, after a long pause, "You, too."

No time to think about what that pause might mean.

11

Liza was thinking about that pause and wondering where it had come from. It was more than something she'd wish for a fellow soldier. She wanted Garret to...what?

Garret—funny how Conway just wouldn't stick anymore—made it a half dozen paces away before he stopped as if he'd been shot. He spun to face her before rushing back. For half a moment she thought he might be coming to kiss her. What reaction that might call for died before it had a chance to be considered as he brushed by her.

"Help me get this guy stripped!" He whipped out a knife and sliced the Afghani's bonds.

"Get undressed," she told him, because she knew what he was after. She took over removing the unconscious man's clothes. Garret was far more powerfully built, but clothes here were loose to fend off the heat. She had all of the man's clothes off and had re-lashed his wrists in case he woke, before turning to offer the clothes to Garret.

Down to his socks and boxers, he was *very much* not the boy she remembered. Muscle rippled over him with every gesture. His job hadn't left him untouched. A long knife scar across his ribs. A bullet wound through one thigh. A spattering of scars that could only come from being caught by a cloud of shrapnel. None of that showed on his face or hands, but his body could only belong to a warrior.

Garret dressed quickly and she did her best not to blush as she helped him, pulling up his *partug* (the blousy pants) and leaving him to figure out how to tie it tightly across his flat stomach while she re-laced his boots. The *khet* over his head, then she was buttoning the cuffs while he tried to settle the draping shirt so that it fell cleanly to his knees.

They kept bumping together in awkward and surprising ways. He couldn't wear his military vest, but the Afghani's vest of brown linen fell past his hips and she was soon ducked under the edge of it to lash Garret's knife's scabbard around one thigh, reaching between his legs to do the lacing.

"A hundred meters," she echoed Mutt's report for him because he'd had to shed his radio to get the pillbox *kufi* hat to sit properly on his head.

She worked her way up his body, tucking sidearms, spare magazines, and grenades where she could. With each oddly intimate contact she became more and more aware of him. When she finished straightening his collar

—he'd made a mess of it—it left her hands holding the narrow collar close about his throat.

Liza leaned in and kissed him for luck. Kissed him for welcoming her in and not holding their past against her. To thank him for giving Rex a merciful death. And to thank him for the man he'd become.

Before he could really respond, she pulled back.

"Fifty meters," she took away his HK416 that instinct had returned to his hands and stuffed an AK-47 into them.

Then she turned him to face the front door.

"Go!" She slapped him on the ass to send him on his way, then she hunkered down in her hiding spot beside Sergey and tried not to laugh at her presumption and his surprise.

"Ready," she whispered to her dog. In moments he was standing and in full alert mode. Nothing would be catching them by surprise.

There were two piles of junk in the back of the long warehouse bay. She shooed Sergey over behind one pile, while she crouched in front of the unconscious man and the two bound women.

Before she could take another breath, Garret had stuck his head out through the black plastic and called out into the night, "*Tsook?*"

12

———

GARRET FELT HE DID A PASSABLE JOB OF EXPLAINING THAT his "good friend" was home sick and had sent him in the man's place.

"Yes, poor Hukam," the man's wife was suddenly beside him.

Even with things happening so fast, Minnow had remembered that the woman was unhappy about the explosives delivery. And now here she was helping him.

"Something he ate," she continued. "It must have come from Pakistan."

In covering his surprise, he glanced away...and spotted his own HK416 in Liza's hands where she peeked around the engine block. It was aimed at the back of the woman's head and Hukam's wife must know it. Okay, maybe she had a couple of reasons to be so cooperative.

Garret turned back and wondered how long the ruse might hold up. Not very long.

"Come. We must hurry. Unload so that you may begin the long drive back. I hope the journey was not too hard."

The leader kept his weapon on Garret, but seemed to agree with the urgency. "You stand aside. We will unload." And he waved the first pickup to back in.

Garret moved to the side wall and was pleased to see that Liza was out of sight, except for a dog tail. Thankfully Sergey wasn't wagging it, but rather standing stock still. Hopefully no one would notice.

Impossible to still think of her as Minnow after that kiss. If she'd wanted him more alert than he'd ever been in his life, she'd figured out how to get him there. Every nuance of that kiss was implanted on his nervous system which was now running at the full-adrenaline setting. He didn't have time to wonder if there was more to that kiss than making sure he was on point, but it had sure as hell worked.

"See?" He tried to distract the leader—and ignore the AK-47 pointed at his gut. "See? We have the car ready." A glance revealed that the incoming supplies were mostly C-4. This was no diesel fuel and fertilizer operation. A lot of money had gone into this effort and they'd stumbled on it because of Liza and her dog.

And the quantity! This many close-packed bricks of C-4 could take down a Parliament building or a Presidential Palace.

A part of him babbled on as if he was extremely proud of his work. Another wished he knew what the hell his team was doing—the lack of radio contact was making him crazy.

Garret tried to keep between the leader and the exposed length of Sergey's tail while the second truck was being unloaded.

13

IF GARRET DIDN'T MOVE SOON, LIZA WAS GOING TO shoot him.

She squatted behind the engine block with the prisoners, which gave her one good line of sight. She'd positioned Sergey near the back door behind the stack of old metal and seats so that the only thing showing past the pile of the truck's fenders was his camera. The two different angles gave her an excellent view of the whole bay—except for Garret being constantly in the way.

Because she was the only one with any idea of what was going on inside the warehouse, she'd become the operation's leader. The fact that she was wholly unqualified didn't seem to matter to the others.

And she couldn't exactly argue, not without being overheard.

So she was answering tactical questions with one tap for yes and two for no.

No, the trucks weren't unloaded yet.

Yes, that really was Garret in the white *khet partug* with the brown vest.

No, not the gray *khet partug* with the white vest.

Yes, with the *kufi* hat.

Yes, it looked remarkably silly on him.

Yes, she wanted to shout. *I will bang your heads together if we get out of this alive.*

No, she didn't have a clear shot on the leader.

Because Garret, you've got to move your ass out of my way.

She looked to Sergey, but he didn't have any ideas either. They were separated by ten feet behind two different piles of junk. Then she noticed that his tail had light on it. Light from one of the trucks shining past the various debris and the engine block.

Very slowly she signaled him out of the light. The view on her wrist screen was now partially blocked by a spare tire, but there was no revealing light hitting Sergey. And the area of the warehouse that Sergey's video feed revealed allowed her to remain hidden, seeing part of the bay with one eye and the dog's angle with the other. She couldn't maintain the split vision for long, but it was enough.

The next time Garret gestured toward something on the truck he glanced back. Then he very deliberately moved aside.

She wanted to kiss him again. He'd been interfering with her picture, because he was trying to protect her dog. He'd seen Sergey's tail and been very careful to block the leader's sightline. That wasn't something a merely good man did. Only a truly wonderful one did something like that.

"I have an idea," Baxter called over the radio. His Pacific Northwest non-accent was a little flatter than Burton's. "Give me a minute."

She could feel Garret's nerves stretching thin as surely as if there was a lead in her hand but connected to Garret rather than Sergey.

In the midst of a sudden clatter from the unloaders, she risked a whispered, "More like twenty seconds."

The second truck was unloaded.

The leader, whose gun was still aimed at Garret, was looking around as if searching for something.

Then Hukam groaned behind her.

The leader twisted her way.

She rolled out into the gap between her engine block hideaway and Sergey's tire and fender pile, and shot the leader in the face over Garret's shoulder. Twice for good measure.

Garret swung free his AK-47 and between them they dropped the other unloaders. The engine roared to life. Then Garret emptied his magazine through the back window of the pickup killing the driver and another guard seated there. The truck lurched halfway out of the bay, then stalled to a stop.

The other two truck engines racketed to life.

"Let the lead driver go," Baxter called out.

There was a harsh blast from the big DShK mounted on the second truck. Stone exploded over her head as rounds from the heavy machine gun pummeled into the warehouse bay. It fired ten, half-inch rounds every second. Rock dust, machine parts, everything seemed to be flying into the air at once.

Then the big gun cut off abruptly as Jeff declared, "Got him!" Thank god for snipers.

Liza risked looking up from where she'd cowered during the fusillade.

"Feh! That's nothing, dude," Mutt transmitted just moments before all hell broke loose.

The Toyota pickup, along with its driver, the DShK, and its dead gunner lifted upward in a massive explosion. BB had planted IEDs out in the yard on just such a chance. Mutt must have triggered one that happened to be directly under the pickup.

The truck shattered. Shrapnel blew into the warehouse bay. Everything that wasn't nailed down blew in her direction.

Once again, flat on the floor, she just prayed that the recently delivered explosives didn't trigger as well.

"Whoops!" Mutt muttered when the explosion had cleared. The entire bay was brightly lit by the truck burning just outside the door. Scorch marks ran halfway down the length of both walls from the tongue of flame that had shot at them. Afghanistan was hot, but the space was now as hot as an oven and for a moment it hurt to breathe.

Garret had rolled under the partially disassembled SUV during the worst of it. Now he rolled back out and turned to look at her. He wore a boy-happy grin on a man's face. There was not even a hint of the dour, glowering boy who had haunted the high school's hallways.

The third truck engine ground gears and raced its engine as it tried to make good its escape. Garret had grabbed the AK-47 from the leader's body and was scrambling toward the door.

"No!" She shouted, remembering that he didn't have a radio. "Baxter said to let it go."

Garret skidded to a halt and looked at her down the length of the bay.

She might have expected confusion, understanding, or surprise on his face. She never expected to see horror.

In that instant, not two feet behind her, she heard the unholy snarl of an enraged Malinois and the scream of a man the moment before his throat was ripped out. She spun just in time to see the steel pipe that Hukam had raised high to smash down on her head fall from nerveless fingers as he tumbled backward under Sergey's onslaught and died.

14

"CHECK IT OUT," BAXTER CLIMBED UP ONTO THE safehouse roof and came over with his laptop.

He held it so that Garret and Liza could see it from where they were sitting side-by-side, leaning back against the roof's balustrade and watching the sunset.

"It worked."

Baxter had dropped down from the roof and ducked out into the open to attach a radio bug under the lead pickup before the firefight had begun—that's why he'd said to let it go. But knowing the Taliban would check for any stray signals, Baxter had set it to turn on after six hours, then deliver only a one-second pulse every ten minutes. Essentially undetectable unless someone was specifically listening for it. The US military had a drone up at forty-thousand feet doing just that.

"Hasn't moved in the last nine hours. Based on the imaging from the drone, I think we have our explosives supplier located."

Garret held up his hand and they traded high-fives. Baxter headed back down the ladder whistling.

Now it was just the three of them, sitting together on the roof of the safehouse—him, Liza, and Sergey with his head happily in her lap. They were just above the line of the protective barriers. High enough to see the great bowl of the Afghan sky, but not high enough to be exposed to any distant snipers on the ground.

Hukam's widow had been very forthcoming on the other caches and local bombmakers she knew around town. She'd hated her husband's fanaticism and had just wanted to live quietly and have a family. With her guidance, Afghan regular forces were going in and clearing out Hukam's former associates.

He wanted to put his arm around Liza. Hold her, pull her in tight. He'd like to—

"Is there a reason you haven't kissed me?" Liza asked the question completely matter-of-factly. She was *so* his kind of woman. Ten years of abandoned, mostly, fantasies and she kept exceeding them at every turn.

"Well, I have to admit, there are a couple."

"What? Do you want your own Kong dog toy and crunchy biscuit?"

"Not so much." He risked putting his arm around her shoulders, because if her question wasn't an invitation to enjoy himself at least that much, he didn't know what was.

Sergey's eyes followed him closely, but he didn't raise his head from her thigh.

Liza leaned into his side and he upgraded to

tightening his arm into a one-armed side embrace. Still no squirm.

"First, that world-class kiss you laid on me was enough to give a man performance anxiety. Could I *ever* return that one appropriately?"

"That's crap, Garret. You were never a man to not trust himself around women. Remember I saw you in the high school halls all those years."

"Maybe I changed."

"Ehhhh!" Liza made a harsh buzzer sound of "total fail."

"Okay, caught me. Two, I know that kiss was in the heat of the moment right before a battle and—"

"Had a lot of experience with pre-battle kisses, have you?"

He couldn't help laughing. "Can't say I have."

"Should I check that with Mutt, or Jeff?"

Garret offered a fake shudder in response. "Both have beards. Ick!"

"So do you."

"But it looks good on me."

"It does," she agreed then continued before he could do more than be surprised. "So what's the real reason?"

"Got two actually. First, this mission is over for us. Out team is moving out tomorrow. Going after that explosives supplier."

"Maybe you should take me there."

"It's way into the worst country you can imagine. Through the heart of Kandahar Province into Lashkar Gah. We did three months there and it makes this place look like a Caribbean resort."

"Maybe you should take me *there* too."

Garret opened his mouth, but nothing came out. He began to wonder if he'd ever keep up with this woman.

"Bet you could use a good dog team in Kandahar."

"Bet we could," he said it slowly and carefully to give himself time to think fast. "You were a huge asset here. We'd have still been checking the first couple warehouse rows when that truck bomb was rebuilt and had crossed the border if it wasn't been for you two." He scratched Sergey's head. His hand came back unmangled, which he'd take as a good sign. In all his years he'd never seen anything like Sergey taking down a man three times his size.

"Bet we could think of something to do together at a Caribbean resort too."

The air whooshed out of him. There was no answer possible to that one. The Minnow in a bikini on a tropical beach—no Baltimore boy could be that lucky, but he could sure hope.

"What's the real reason you haven't kissed me?"

Garret smiled at her. He just couldn't help himself. As easily as he could imagine Minnow in a beach bikini, he could imagine Liza Minot in a beach wedding dress. The craziest and best part was that he could imagine himself standing right there beside her, feet planted in the sand, with a dog for a ringbearer.

"The real reason..." he trailed it out.

"Uh-huh," she looked up at him with those perfect blue eyes that he never wanted to look away from.

"I don't think Sergey would like it much."

Liza leaned down and tickled the dog's ears. "What do

you think? After all, he's not quite the arrogant master sergeant we thought he was. Maybe we need to come up with a command past 'Friend'."

Sergey inspected him balefully for a long moment before heaving one of his dog sighs as if giving in to the inevitable. He shifted his position so that his back lay along her thigh, but he was now looking out at the desert. Apparently it was okay with him, but he'd rather not watch.

"Well," Liza looked up at him and Garret could feel his heart pick up the pace. "I guess Sergey doesn't really mind. And I most certainly don't."

As he leaned in to kiss her, Garret still kept one eye on the dog.

PLAY THE RIGHT CARDS

Ramiro dreams a simple dream: become a great chef to capture the heart of the best cook he ever met. Now, in just-next-door restaurants in their old neighborhood—the barrios of Medellín, Colombia—he brings a modern twist to catch her attention.

Estela's worries center on the last gasp of the drug cartels that still haunt her neighborhood. When a pair of American Delta operators start a card game in Ramiro's restaurant, she wonders if she too can Play the Right Cards.

INTRODUCTION

This story happened because of an escalator.

No, really!

The city of Medellín, Colombia had atrocious problems. It had been the center of Pablo Escobar's drug-running empire, and his terror war against other cartels and the government itself until his death in 1993.

In the last twenty years, the population has grown from two million to almost four million people. And that massive urbanization has occurred mostly due to the agglomeration of slums around the periphery and the less desirable mountaintops that surround the city.

The commute for the service personnel from the slums to the prosperous core could easily take an hour or more, despite often being less than a kilometer apart as the crow flies. Roads were indirect, and transit was nearly non-existent. Essentially, commerce didn't occur across a distance of a few dozen blocks.

So the city installed an escalator.

A thousand feet long, it connected one of the poorest slums to the city below in a matter of minutes.

Medellín didn't stop there. Gondola systems were installed. Libraries were built at the upper end of the anchor points of the system to make them more attractive to visitors and instill pride in the locals. These and other improvements have allowed development capital to flow uphill and services to flow down.

What happens then?

Change happens.

The city has become an international model for innovative urban-interconnection solutions. Is it all perfect? Of course not, but it is a vast amount of progress, especially when compared to Escobar's personal fiefdom.

To exemplify this change, I fell back on one of my favorite things—food. I put two restaurants side by side: one deeply traditional, one madly innovative.

So I had most of a setting.

Yet I also wanted to show the hard uphill battle (both literally and figuratively) that the city still had ahead of them.

Escobar's empire was broken, but seventy percent of the world's cocaine comes from Colombia. And a legacy as deep and intrusive as Escobar's doesn't disappear overnight, or even in the years since his death.

How convenient that I had just finished my Delta Force romance novel series.

Chad and Duane, a particularly lethal pair of operators from that series, always brought a sense of fun with them.

So, in this gloriously messy, mixed-up, changing, dangerous, exciting heart of Medellín, they helped our hero and heroine find a new future.

1

___

The flash of white-gold drew Ramiro's attention from the *mote de queso.*

It was a soup he'd lifted from Colombia's Caribbean Coast and was adapting to the Medellín palate—with his own modern style of course. The thick hard cheese had been transformed to tiny floating islands that would catch in every spoonful. The sweetness of yam now came from roasted and juiced corn, and the coconut milk base was reconstructed from goat milk and white chocolate.

It was close. So close. It needed more roasted-corn milk—and, he tried not to sigh, less salt. Nowhere in Colombia was there a love for the salt and sweet together as there was in Medellín, but the balance was wrong. The only way to put less in was to start over and he'd already been nursing this soup along for two days. Any distraction was welcome.

The flash of white-gold was a man's pale blond hair. Not exactly common in the heart of the Santo Domingo district of Medellín. It belonged to a big guy. Tall and incredibly broad of shoulder. The man who followed him in was darker, but no smaller. They looked like two tanks rolling into his restaurant. Ramiro didn't need to be brilliant to spot American drug-war military.

"*Buenos días, amigos.* Welcome to my restaurant." He worked hard on his English hoping for just this moment. American military liked to think they were adventurous, but they rarely were. It had taken three months for one to walk in here. If he could make a good impression, they'd tell their friends and then he'd be made. The *barrio*'s locals were fine, but money came from the Americans. Also if the Americans came, then the trendy Paisas from lower Medellín would start riding the tram or the escalator up into the *barrio* and they too had money.

"Hey there." The blond man offered one of those odd, meaningless American greetings as they looked around.

The *barrio* of Santo Domingo had changed so much since the days when Pablo Escobar's drug money had ruled here, that the neighborhood of his youth was almost unrecognizable. There were still alleys and streets that even he didn't walk into, but no longer did everyone spend whole days cowering out of sight as gun battles raged along the *Fronteras Invisibles* that had divided the drug militias' territories. With new parks, libraries, civic centers, and even massive outdoor escalators that climbed right up into the hills of the upper *comunas,* the neighborhoods had slowly quieted and were regaining cohesion, like a fine sauce.

It wasn't done yet, but gunfire was now less common than bombs had been the year when six thousand had died in this city alone. The lower city was far safer and the hill neighborhoods were following.

Ramiro had done his best to make his restaurant fit the modern times. The walls were white, with paintings of local vistas—cheap ones from street artists but with a sharp, modernist eye. The tables were topped with black Formica and dark blue linoleum covered the old wood floors. The chairs he'd selected for comfort over style. This restaurant was his very breath, and his future.

"Would you like some lunch, my friends?" Please let them be his friends. He moved out to escort them to seats. There were ten tables and only two were occupied, so where they sat didn't matter; the secret was to get them sitting.

"Sure. Duane says he's ready to eat a horse. Me, I'm fine with just a small cow or two." Their Spanish was very good, though strangely regionless. It didn't matter, it made his life easier. He still had to concentrate to get English syntax organized in his head before he spoke.

When he tried to hand over menus, the blond guy waved them away. "You're the chef, you choose. We're not picky eaters."

"*I'm* not," 'Duane' grumbled out in a voice that sounded little used. "Chad's got this thing against *aji chombo* sauce."

"Only because the last time you said 'Try it, you'll like it,' it burned a hole in my tongue that came out through the bottom of my boots. I liked those boots."

"He likes wearing ballet slippers."

Ramiro knew it was bad form to laugh in a customer's

face—especially one he wanted to turn into a repeat customer—but he couldn't help himself.

"That's ballet *dancers.* Those girls bring a whole new meaning to flexible. And I won't mention Duane and his bunny slippers," blond 'Chad's' smile forgave Ramiro his laugh.

Ramiro wasn't sure what "bunny slippers" were. He wondered if they used their real names. Probably. Duane's tan was dark enough, but Chad would never pass as undercover anything in Colombia. Time to get back to the food.

"The reason you don't like the *aji chombo* is because you eat the Venezuelan sauce." Venezuela was just another confirmation of who they were as it was a border that was not very comfortable to cross right now. "You must try my *aji picante Colombiano.* It is hot, but it is not simply hot with peppers. It is hot with *flavor.* It is hot with the spirit of Colombia."

"Bring it on, brother." Duane turned to his friend, "You got the cards?"

"You were supposed to— Shit, bro." He turned to Ramiro. "Do you have any playing cards?"

Ramiro went to look, but all he found were a pack of My Little Pony cards his niece had left behind on her last visit from Bogota.

"Sorry, all I could find, my friends."

Chad fanned the deck. Ramiro should have told them he couldn't find anything. They'd take offense at these silly pink cards and walk away.

Brightly colored cartoon ponies adorned them. The suits were made up of hearts, diamonds, rainbows, and more. A "three of butterflies" flew around the image of Fluttershy, a beige pony with hot pink hair. A "seven of balloons" floated above the wild-eyed party pony Pinkie Pie with her hot pink hair. He and Marie had played the game for endless hours. Those days had gone by far too fast. No little girl of his own to raise. No little boy to follow in his footsteps. Not yet anyway, but Marie made him wish.

But these military men were not eight-year old Marie.

It was a disaster before he'd even served the first plate. They'd never come back. He—

Chad quickly chucked aside the eights, nines, and tens, then began shuffling the deck. Truco? Two American military men were going to play a vicious, cut-throat game like Truco with My Little Pony cards.

They seemed to forget about his existence, so he slowly eased away and almost landed in Jesús Rivera's lap, which would have been very bad. He'd known Jesús since they were kids, but his was the last major drug militia still working Santo Domingo. He'd become so hard over the years that Ramiro had barely recognized him when he returned from his apprenticeship and cooking school in Bogotá.

Ramiro hurried back to the kitchen.

2

___

Estela had watched the Americans stroll past the front of her restaurant without thinking anything of it. But when news had spread—as quickly as everything in the *barrio* did—of a noisy two-person game of Truco in Ramiro's *Restaurante de Medellín*, she had her suspicions. When Marla came in for an order of *chicharrón* with a side of beans and rice to take to her ailing father—who had made a profession of ailing ever since his daughter had married well enough to support him—and asked how it was possible for hair to be so close to white on a young and handsome man, it only confirmed what Estela already knew.

The Americans wanted to eat at Ramiro's? It was their loss. It wasn't authentic Colombian food. It was barely food according to some of her customers. She didn't need more customers. Even Ramiro returning from the big city with his big city ideas and moving in next door hadn't worried her.

The *Paisas* of Medellín—the real locals—knew real

food. She and Cara could barely keep up with the crowded tables. Those who had to wait were always offered a *jugó* of iced juice mixed with coconut milk. She knew the feeding and keeping of customers far better than Ramiro with his fancy molecules and *espuma* that he dropped in frothy little piles as if a person could be satisfied with air and bubbles.

He knew nothing.

Then why did the Americans eating there irk her so?

She paused in the kitchen long enough to drink a lime and coconut *jugó* herself as the thin-sliced plantain *patacones* fried for the second time. Her *restaurante* was warm compared to Ramiro's chilly *moderno* nonsense. The wood walls had been placed here by her grandfather. Her grandmother had fed the people of Santo Domingo at these same wooden tables. Even when Pablo Escobar and the other murderous drug scum had ruled the streets, people still had to eat.

She had learned that lesson to her very soul on the day that a bomb killed her mother as she walked along the street with a basket of chicken and potatoes. The explosion had also killed the children of a police captain. It was the day that Estela's schooling *and* childhood had ended. She and Nana had run the restaurant from the very next day, *because the people they must eat, si?* Now this place was hers. No, it was *her.* She and her restaurant were one and the same. It was something else she had learned from Nana.

She didn't need Ramiro. She didn't care about his food that wasn't food. And she certainly didn't miss the few people who went to his restaurant when hers was crowded for hours every mealtime.

"What's on the menu today, Estela?" She knew the voice without turning.

"Nothing for you, Jesús Rivera. Ever. I told you not to come in here." She rattled the basket in the frying oil.

"Why don't you like me, Estela? I can show you a very good time. Take you away from all this sweaty work. All these people." *All these people* was precisely why she was here. She loved serving traditional, hearty food to the *Paisas* of Medellín.

She had told him a thousand times no. They had all grown up together here: her, Ramiro, Jesús, and so many others. Many were dead in the drug wars, some had left, very few had come back like Ramiro. She had thought him long gone and wished him well away. It was only after he left that she'd come to miss him. He had been a young man of dreams.

Jesús had just become a runner for the local drug militia back then—still called Pablo's Domingo Guerrilleros even after Escobar's death. Jesús' *compañeros*, though, had boasted loudly of killing the police captain's children. All of her begging had brought no police to the *barrio* seeking justice. She had even gone to Jesús as a friend. At the age of fourteen, he had tried to set the price for helping her as having his way with her. When she had refused, he had slapped her face so hard that it had hurt for a week. She'd given him his first knife scar in payback. Jesús was now the Guerrilleros' leader.

He would be leaning on the small service counter that separated her kitchen from the crowd. Everyone would be watching, of course. The rapidly quieting restaurant all remembered how she and Jesús had run together as children. She wondered how much money had changed hands over the years betting on if, or when, Jesús would bed her.

Not now. Not ever.

She dipped the empty wire basket deep in the frying oil and tipped her head for several seconds as if considering how to respond to him. The restaurant was stone silent now in anticipation of her answer, but that couldn't be helped.

Yanking the basket from the oil, she tapped it once to clear the drips before whirling on him to hold it less than an inch from his smug face. His smugness disappeared fast enough.

"The answer, Jesús, is that there is *nothing* on the menu here for you. Not me, not a bowl of *mondongo* soup, not a glass of juice. If you come in my restaurant again, you will wear a seared print of this basket on your face until the end of your days."

He held her gaze and she wondered how crazy a risk she'd just taken.

They held each other's glare until a single drip of hot oil fell from the basket onto the back of his hand where it rested on the counter.

His yelp of surprise and jerk backwards elicited a laugh from the gathered diners. Jesús gave her a look darker than the ancient iron of her grill and stalked out the door. A hubbub of speculations among the diners washed across the tables. Some thought it was the next step in an on-going courtship. Others felt that it was proof that it was all decided for now and ever. Only one or two eyed her with caution.

Yes, if they were smart, they would stay away for a while. There was no doubt in her mind, the worst was yet to come.

As she returned to her cooking, she considered her options, but they were few and far between. She was alone now. Oh, she had many friends in the community, but most of those were smart enough to still fear Jesús Rivera and the remains of the Domingo Guerrilleros. Her grandmother had died of old age, her father during an accident in the oil fields, and her mother by that bomb.

Who could help her?

The scene with her and Jesús complete, at least for now, conversation slowly shifted back to speculating about the two men eating at Ramiro's. They fit none of the standard tourist stereotypes except for being American and where they chose to eat. That implied they were US military.

There was no question, at least not in the hilltop *barrios* of Medellín, that it had been America's Delta Force who finally took down Escobar. The trademark sharpshooting was proof enough, even without what those on the street had seen. The Colombian police had tried—at least the ones not too afraid of retribution had tried—but the shot to the head as Pablo had raced across uneven roof tiles was too neat, too perfect. And the small American team who had been haunting Medellín for months had disappeared that night.

The two Americans. They weren't merely US military.

Delta Force was back in Santo Domingo. If there was anyone to stop Jesús, they were the men to do it.

How to get their attention?

She was pretty enough to get any man's attention—Jesús had only been one of the many who followed her about in their youth and since. But there was a *far* more reliable way to get any man's attention, especially the kind of attention she wanted.

3

———

"Hey, Ramiro. You still got that girlie deck of cards?"

Ramiro looked up in delight. He hadn't expected the Americans to come back the very next day. And for dinner, which was even better than lunch. His ploy had worked. He had cooked for them like he'd never cooked before—though he wished he hadn't given in to the temptation to serve his salty soup. It was the only dish they had neither remarked on nor finished.

"Dickhead forgot them again," Chad hooked a thumb over his shoulder, but no one was there. Duane must be outside, maybe with more of their friends.

"Sure, here you go, *mi amigo.*" He tossed the pack over the counter.

"Thanks. I'll get them back to you."

Ramiro could only gawk in surprise as Chad strode back out the door. Ramiro hurried past the few diners lingering over dessert and looked out just in time to see Chad turn into Estela's restaurant.

"*No! Imposible!*" He couldn't breathe against the pressure in his chest. How had that woman bewitched *his* Americans? The same way she'd bewitched him and every other person in all Santo Domingo since she'd learned to walk. He'd become a cook to impress her. And when that hadn't worked, he'd left and studied to become a chef. He had taken over the building next door to hers so that he could show her just who could cook now. Not that she seemed to be succumbing to his grand plan.

But to steal his Americans was beyond unfair.

Cara, her waitress, stepped out the front door to set some folding chairs and a card table on the sidewalk in front of Estela's restaurant. With the hot sun setting, it would be as cool and inviting here as the inside of her restaurant had always been. The Garcia family stepped out of the restaurant and sat at the table—all seven of them crowded together. That would be a nice ticket, even at Estela's low prices. He glanced in through the small window. The place teemed with people. His Americans were in a corner near the kitchen, completely out of reach, wielding his niece's My Little Pony cards as if they were weapons of war. Their game of Truco now had numerous spectators.

Estela came out balancing great platters of empanadas and salsas for the Garcias. Only as she finished serving them did she turn and see him.

"Ramiro," she offered him one of those amazing, friendly smiles that made him forgive her everything.

Except this time.

He steeled his inner resolve, but could only manage one word.

"How?" he waved a hand toward the window.

Her lovely brow furrowed for only a moment. "Oh. The Delta Force men."

"They're not—" But Estela had always been the smartest *chica* in school, until the day she had to leave to work here. If she said that's what they were, they must be. "*Si.* Them."

"I offered them each one of my *obleas* for dessert when they left your restaurant yesterday, then invited them to come back the next time they were hungry."

"That's not fair, Estela." Nobody made an *oblea* as good as Estela. Each wafer was bigger around than the tips of his spread fingers and thinner than a whisper. She built them in layers of jam, then wafer, then salty white cheese, another wafer, thickened cream, and so on until they were an inch thick. Sweet, salty, thick, crunchy—it was every possible flavor and texture in each delicate bite.

She gave him an unreadable look.

"You know what this means, don't you?" And he stalked back to his own restaurant. If it was war she wanted, he'd bring it and bring it hard.

4

———

Estela watched Ramiro go and tried not to feel the ache in her heart. He had been so strange since his return that in some ways she no longer knew him. Where was the boy whose eyes had followed her even when he himself hadn't dared? It had taken her until he had left to understand that perhaps the quiet boy was the good one and the ones who were so brash and confident— especially those waving about their drug wealth—were *not* so kind. But now?

Now Ramiro would barely speak with her. And somehow, her seeking the protection of the Americans was yet another offense. She would have to do something about that—when she didn't have a restaurant crowded with customers and Jesús to worry about.

The dinner service ran by so fast as it always did when she was busy. She was outside in the soft twilight, cleaning up the dishes when a hand grabbed her wrist forcing her to drop a plate that shattered on the rough street. She knew it immediately by the long, thin cruelty of the fingers that her cheek still remembered from all those years ago.

"It's time, *chica*," Jesús breathed in her ear as his other hand clamped about her waist from behind. "It is time you finally gave me what is mine."

She was helpless against his whipcord strength.

His hand shifted over her mouth. She tried to bite it, but he was expecting that and merely wrenched her neck harder as he forced her to walk ahead of him down the street.

He was going to rape her in some back alley. And she was going to fight until he was forced to kill her to do so. For all her struggles, she might as well have been a fly to be shooed away from a hock of raw lamb.

Tears began to stream down her face. To end like this was too horrible for thought. If she could die right here, right now, shredded by a bomb like her mother, she would take that over what awaited her at Jesús' hands.

Then, by some miracle, it happened. She was slammed down onto the street. But she wasn't dead. Her ears didn't bleed from the blast of the bomb.

At the sound of the snarl behind her, she rolled over and saw Jesús' back. And beyond him she saw the two Delta men.

"Looky here, buddy," the blond one had his hands tucked into his back pockets. "We've got someone who isn't playing nice. He's trying to take away the chef before we get another one of her *obleas*."

"Doesn't seem right," the darker one agreed. There was a gun in his hand, but he was holding it oddly. More as if he'd snatched it out of Jesús' waistband than if he'd pulled his own from some hidden spot. With three gestures so fast that she couldn't follow them, he separated the gun into four pieces. He pocketed one piece, threw a pair of them into a garbage can, and chucked the last into one of the neighborhood's brand new storm drains where it rattled away.

Jesús yanked out a knife and flicked it open. She wanted to warn them, he was an expert knife fighter, just as his father had been when he was one of Escobar's actual bodyguards. But the cry caught in her throat. She had scarred Jesús' face with that knife when she was twelve. And now he was going to carve up these men whose help she needed but hadn't had time to ask.

And then he was going to carve her.

"Aw, ain't he cute," the blond one had no idea the danger he was in. "He's got a pig sticker."

"More like a guinea pig sticker," the darker one answered.

"Maybe it's a mouse sticker."

Neither man had the sense to reach for a gun. If they really were Delta Force, they must have guns.

The next moment happened so fast, she could never quite make sense of it.

"Pitiful, dude," the blond one sounded bored and walked by Jesús as if he wasn't even there. He bent down to offer her his hand with his back to the most dangerous knife fighter in the *barrio*, perhaps in Medellín.

Jesús moved to take advantage.

Before she could scream a warning, the darker one stepped forward. One moment Jesús was lunging with his knife. The next he was pinned with his back against the wall, his feet off the ground, and the only sound in the night was his knife clattering down upon a stone. His knife hand was clutched tightly in his other hand as if it was in great pain.

"Little boys shouldn't play with knives," the blond one winked at her as he helped her to her feet, only then turning to see what had happened.

With no apparent effort, the darker one lifted Jesús clear of the wall, then tossed him into the same garbage can where parts of his gun had been thrown.

The blond one picked up the blade and inspected it carefully.

"A gift from Escobar to his father," she told him.

"A custom Terzuola. One of his early designs. Make for a good souvenir."

"He was generous with his men." There were still people who worshipped Escobar. He had brought the first lights to a Medellín soccer field so that the locals could play at night. He gave gifts to his adherents so that they lived like kings. And threw lavish parties for "his people"—the *Paisas* of the *barrio*.

"And lethal to his enemies." The blond folded the blade back into the handle with a practiced flick then offered it to her.

She shook her head. "I want no part of the past. Medellín is better with his death. The narco-tourists—they should all live as I did. All die as my mother did. Then we would see if they think it is so fascinating."

He nodded, instead tossing her the deck of brightly cheerful cards they'd been using to play Truco. "Could you make sure these get back to Ramiro?" They walked her back to her restaurant, waved, and disappeared into the night.

Estela was done with the past. In so many ways.

She looked in, saw that Cara was almost done cleaning the restaurant. When she waved through the window, she received a cheery wave back. No one was the wiser for tonight's events, which was a blessing.

The bright lights still streamed out onto the rough pavement from *Restaurante de Medellín.* She stepped into that bright light, then into Ramiro's restaurant. She had never actually been in here. She didn't understand the stark colors and sharp edges, but she'd seen his prices and his clientele dressed in their expensive clothes.

"Is this the future?" She wondered aloud.

Ramiro twisted around from where he was resetting a last table, making sure the linen tablecloth—an actual tablecloth—was arranged just so.

5

———

"One version of it." Ramiro could feel the bitterness in his voice, but it was hard to feel it when he looked at her. She wore the simplest of clothes, a voluminous red skirt in her grandmother's village's pattern that she made beautiful rather than mundane. Her white blouse, its collar and sleeves embroidered with tiny red roses, hung loosely over her generous figure until it gathered in the skirt at her trim waist. Her long dark hair framed a face so lovely that Prieto might have painted it, if Estela hadn't so brought so much life to it herself.

Her eyes seemed a little wider than usual, as if she'd just been running and was surprised to find herself breathless.

"Feed me your food, Ramiro. Show me what it is you do."

In a dream, he pulled aside a seat for her and held it out.

She shook her head, her hair now loose rather than in the generous ponytail he'd seen earlier, she moved up to the counter facing the kitchen to sit at one of the stools. She made a show of placing two napkins—one in front of her and one at the stool beside her, then set down the deck of My Little Pony playing cards.

"They're gone?"

She nodded.

He searched for anger, but couldn't seem to find it.

He started with the soup he had rebuilt from scratch. It was still young—two more days simmering and the broth would truly meld—but the salt and the sweet, the fruit and the cheese were finally in the right balance.

She tasted. With her soft sigh as encouragement, he moved on to rock shrimp steamed in hearts of palm with a pineapple foam. Shaved New York strip served on yucca bread with liquid nitrogen crystalized guacamole shards and seared discs of *chicharón*. She said nothing, but she finished everything down to the last fork-clattering scrape of the plate. The meal stretched long into the night as he made only one course and two plates at a time, then sat to share it with her. Only when they were done, did he rise to start the next course.

Finally he made dessert—his version of an *oblea*.

The wafer was seasoned with fine-grated candied ginger and the tiniest shreds of dark-roasted habanero and red bell pepper so that it almost sparkled with color. He had deconstructed the elements of salt and sweet, savory and umami, *crema de leche* and merest slivers of aged ham. He had stayed up through the night using all of his skills to create it, to win the Americans back from Estela. Never in a thousand years had he imagined that he would be making it for her instead. He served it on a clean white plate in neatly sliced pie sections rather than the traditional full round wrapped in foil.

When he served it on the single plate and set it between their places, it felt as if all the life had gone out of him. He couldn't even find the energy to lift a slice for himself. Instead, he sat and watched as Estela bit off the end of one of the slices with her perfect white teeth. She closed her eyes as she chewed and, he hoped, savored.

She set it down after only the one lone bite.

"You don't like it." She had always been the best cook he'd ever known. They had sung his praises in Bogotá, but none of that mattered. What mattered was what Estela thought. And she had set it down after one bite.

Then she slipped a finger under his chin and forced him to look up at her. It might be the first time they had ever touched.

"How?"

How had he failed? He didn't know. "I was trying—" *foolishly* "—to impress you. That was always why I cooked. You remember how my father would beat me, but I never let you know why. It was because I wouldn't join a cartel and take the easy drug money, instead I cooked. For you."

Her thumb brushed his cheek so gently.

If he was any less of a man, he would cry. But he had his pride, and that didn't include crying in front of Estela. He would leave. He would take the remains of his meager savings and go back to Bogotá. There he would open a restaurant in the finest neighborhood where they understood him, rather than some *barrio* where he no longer belonged.

Her kiss was flavored with his *oblea.*

Estela's lips were softer and warmer than he'd ever imagined. They were like her cooking, so complete and perfect that he didn't know why he'd ever even tried to compete.

She eased back ever so slightly, but still her hand was on his cheek.

"It was amazing, Ramiro. You captured the flavors of the *Paisa*—the flavor of the people—but somehow you brought it a new life without losing the heart of the food. And I will never make another *oblea* when I could have one of yours instead."

"It was all for you, Estela. You're the only thing I ever wanted."

She smiled. "I understand that now." And she leaned back in for another kiss.

He closed his eyes just as their lips met and—

A hand grabbed him by the scruff of the neck and tossed him aside. He crashed into the line of stools and landed in a painful tangle on the floor.

"Don't be taking what's mine, Ramiro. You know better than that."

Jesús Rivera tipped up a stool and dropped into it beside Estela. He reached out with a hand and grabbed a fistful of Estela's hair, but hissed with pain as if she had spikes in it.

"Hand hurting, Jesús?" Estela's sarcasm earned her a sharp slap across the jaw with the back of his other hand.

"No *Americano* here to protect you now."

And Ramiro understood.

Estela hadn't been trying to steal his Americans. She

had recognized Delta Force operators and gambled that they were the only ones skilled enough to take on Jesús. He had not become the leader of Pablo's Domingo Guerrilleros with his gentle ways—he'd left a trail of the scarred, the crippled, and the dead in the wake of his success.

But they weren't here now.

Ramiro tried to move silently, but was too tangled in the stools.

"Get me something to drink." Jesús didn't even bother to turn. Neither did he release his fistful of Estela's hair.

Ramiro could feel Estela's eyes on him as he stepped through the gap in the counter and found a bottle of Aguardiente. Ramiro of the past would have served it in a glass. Would have scurried away and tried not to think about what Jesús did to his women.

But that was a Ramiro he no longer knew. Estela had kissed him. Had told him without words that she loved his food. And that maybe, just maybe she had real feelings for him.

He uncorked the bottle and set it on the counter by Jesús. He could see Estela's eyes die a little as Ramiro backed away. As Jesús would expect.

Backed away, while Jesús twisted Estela's head cruelly one way and another. Backed away until his hand landed exactly where he intended, on the ten-inch chef's knife that he always put in the same precise spot on his counter.

By shifting behind Jesús, he blocked Estela's view of him. Then, lunging through the server's gap in the counter, he plunged the knife into Jesús' back. It was like plunging it into stone. The shock slammed up his arm as Jesús roared in fury. He spun on Ramiro as the small stream of blood ran down from his shoulder blade.

Stupid. He should have thought about a man's anatomy. Where were you supposed to stab a man? How would he know? In the kidneys might have been good if he had thought of it in time. Instead his knife had bounced off Jesús' shoulder blade and only infuriated him.

His punch slammed Ramiro back against his stove; the pain such an explosion that he could only collapse to the floor.

Jesús was also screaming in pain, holding his hand close to his chest. But his face was almost black with rage. Jesús bent down to pick up the knife that the force of Ramiro's attack had knocked out of his hand. There was no question he was about to die on his own blade.

Unwilling to witness his own death, he squeezed his eyes shut against the coming blow.

Then he heard a deep voice. "Thought we told you that little boys shouldn't play with knives."

Jesús' roared with fury. Ramiro opened his eyes and managed to lean far enough to look through the counter's gap. The Americans caught Jesús' charge as if he was a butterfly on one of the My Little Pony cards.

"Didn't realize you were Jesús Rivera," Chad continued. "Been looking for you for a bit. Might have saved these folks some trouble if you'd bothered to introduce yourself earlier. Excuse us." He offered both Estela and him pleasant nods as if they were passing each other on the street.

They marched Jesús out the door and into the night.

Rumors sprang up of magnificent final gun battles or dark American prisons, but no one ever saw Jesús Rivera again.

Ramiro and Estela had kept their thoughts to themselves.

Months later, Ramiro could only wonder at Estela's brilliance. She had been right as usual. He had wanted to cut a wide arch between their restaurants, but Estela had only let him cut a window between their kitchens. It was enough of an opening that he could see her cooking whenever he wanted to, but not so much that their restaurants would merge as their lives had.

She'd insisted that what he did was art compared to her simple food. But he never doubted that comfort food was what kept a *Paisa* happy. "To protect your art, there must be a wall between us," she'd insisted. But it was the only part of their lives that stayed separate. She had married him and soon they would have their first child.

And the Americans had come. Sometimes to one restaurant, sometimes to the other. They often brought their friends, which had attracted others, both military and from the city center. Their restaurants had thrived.

But there were only two things that ever passed through the small window between their kitchens.

Estela had insisted that he provide a constant supply of his "magnificent" *obleas* for her customers as well as his own.

And the deck of My Little Pony playing cards, depending on which restaurant the Americans came to eat and play wild games of Truco.

CARRYING THE HEART'S LOAD

Delta Force Captain "Killer Kristine" knows how to carry the load, right down to her very bones. Yanking some scientist out of a Venezuela prison is just another burden to bear.

But the man she rescues is no average nerd. His tough questions force her to face how long she's been carrying that load. And just what's possible if she could ever set it down.

INTRODUCTION

This story was written on a challenge. My friend Blaze Ward is also an anthology editor. He created an antho titled *An Interpretation of Moles.* He then invited about a dozen of us to come up with crazy and innovative stories about moles.

A mole is:

- a measurement in atomic chemistry
- a feature that sometimes appears on the skin
- a small brown furry critter
- a Mexican chocolate-based sauce
- ...a fun, multifarious word.

Of course, being me, I decided to use all of those and more.

But still, all I had was a word, I needed a story.

As I was contemplating this story, I happened to be reading yet another article about President Maduro of Venezuela finding new ways to destroy his own country, starve his people, and blame it all on anyone else he could, especially the US.

That a country with so much bounty is dying at his hands is beyond criminal. Curiosity led me to poke around a little. If international forces actually were to invade Venezuela to depose him, what would they be up against?

One of the things that caught my eye was a pretty little (57') patrol boat built in the US. Just perfect. If the US military ever did go into Venezuela, they'd be facing some of their own hardware.

Which sounded like a job for Delta Force.

Add in one of the US's very worst Superfund sites—so bad that they still haven't figured out how to clean it up even though it was one of the first named sites and lies in the heart of Brooklyn—and I had my story of moles.

1
———

"Gonna be a cakewalk, Captain Killer Kristine."

"Pretty arrogant for someone who doesn't have a clue, Mankowski." She'd be damned if she'd call him by his first name. And being the only woman in the squad, there was no way she was using Master Sergeant Connie "Girlie" Mankowski's tag. Having "Girlie" be her only other option just wasn't going down.

Command must have it in for her. Actually, Command notoriously had it in for all Delta Force operators but she seemed to draw the short end of the stick a hell of a lot—or maybe it was the electrified end.

"Hey," Mankowski protested as he rewrapped his MREs. "I'm not arrogant. I'm awesome." A Delta operator who liked to talk too much—and of course he ended up on her team.

They were both sitting on the hangar deck of the USS *Peleliu* helicopter carrier doing the standard mission prep. Last she'd heard, this ship had been decommissioned.

But here it was as big as life, a secret floating base for the Night Stalkers Spec Ops helicopter guys. Too bad the air jocks couldn't do shit to help on this one except dump them five klicks off the Venezuelan coast and wish them luck.

Standard mission prep included pre-dissecting their Meals-Ready-to-Eat. With a little judicious opening and culling, they could cut down the volume-per-meal they'd have to carry in their packs by as much as fifty percent and mass by thirty percent. Wrap the retained meal packets in a strip of hundred-mile-an-hour duct tape and they were good to go. Every kilo less food equaled an additional pair of thirty-round magazines for her HK416 rifle or five seventeen-round mags for her Glock sidearm.

The mission was only supposed to be ten hours. The last one-night mission she'd been on had gone for five days, so she packed enough food for two people to last three days as a compromise.

"I've walked Syria and Afghanistan. This ain't no worse." Like he was trying to impress her.

She was so immune to that crap. Her big brother had thought she was an ideal playground, until she'd nutted him so hard that he hadn't walked right for a week. That had set the tone of her life. Uncle Juan, Steve who'd missed a whole season of high school football because she'd had to shatter his foot to back him off, three guys she'd left bloody in Brooklyn, and five she'd left dead out in the Congo.

That had been another fine command decision, Puerto Rican dark didn't pass for African black anywhere except in the two-tone colorblindness of America—white and not. Sure as hell hadn't passed her in the Congo. This time at least they were sending her into Venezuela, so her skin would be okay, if not her accent. Of course Mankowski was a Chicago white boy—target right on his fucking face—she was so screwed.

"Besides, walking beside a hot number like Killer Kristine, nobody's going to be looking at this old boy anyway. I'm safe as can be."

Kristine wondered who was going to kill this guy first, her or the nightmare that was modern-day Venezuela.

It was a bum assignment anyway: walk into a major military base in an exceptionally paranoid country, find idiot scientist, extract him out of whatever shitstorm political hole he'd gotten himself stuck in, and make sure he comes back alive and in one piece. Command had really stressed the alive and intact part of the mission—while being equally careful to not say one word about what condition men like Girlie Mankowski had to be in upon their return. Or her for that matter. But they were hella concerned about one Dr. Ray Ewing.

You know, he's one of "those" kind of scientists, her mission briefer had said.

Yeah, and you're one of "those" kind of briefers who would be clearly happy to eat his own shit and spew it back out again.

One of "those" scientists? Absentminded, unworldly, or just an arrogant know-it-all pain-in-the-ass? She *so* couldn't wait to find out which.

"Where you from, Killer?"

"Hell."

"No really."

She stopped slit-packing MREs and looked at him until he stopped opening his and faced her.

"What?"

"Hell. Really."

2

Once she was done with organizing meals, water, and ammo, she started considering how she was supposed to extract a civilian alive. She sure wasn't going to give him a weapon; he'd be as likely to shoot himself or her rather than the bad guys. But she stuffed one in her pack just in case by some miracle of Mother Mary he *did* know which end to hold it by.

She didn't wear issued armor. Between the weight and freedom of movement issues, she typically wore no more than a Dragonskin vest—even if it wasn't official issue. It worked better and weighed a quarter of the fully-plated Improved Outer Tactical Vest with its heavy ceramic plates, it just wasn't politically correct. But then she wasn't either. This time, she'd layer up with both Dragonskin and the heavy armor of the IOTV, then she'd let the eminent Dr. Ewing wear the heavy shit on the return leg.

Over that, she pulled on her MOLLE. The Modular Lightweight Load-carrying Equipment was a fancy way to say a harness vest. Its entire surface was covered with inch-wide horizontal straps, spaced an inch apart. Every Delta operator's was unique because it was wholly configurable. The base MOLLE—pronounced Molly—carried eight magazines. Then various holders of the PALS—Pouch Attachment Ladder System—were added on to an individual's preference. The various pouches interlaced through the straps in such a way that you could probably do a helicopter hoist extraction by any of them, though it had the ring on the front for that.

A lot of operators put the med kit on the very back of their rucksack—*Not gonna need it anyway.* She kept it front and center so that she didn't have to dump her pack to access it every time she was patching up some asshole who was too injured to reach the kit on their back, or worse, had dumped their pack in order to survive an op gone bad. Flares, breaching charges, timers, hydration bladder, extra mags for her sidearm and ankle piece, satellite radio, backup radio, batteries...the list was endless of what she wanted to carry. And now she had to dump half of it so that she could carry gear for some civilian who'd probably bitch the whole way.

Girlie Mankowski only whined a little about how much of it there was, but took his share after she offered to remove his pelvis with the Benchmade Infidel blade she wore in a wrist sheath if he said another word.

"Just jokin', man," he muttered to himself.

By some mutual agreement, she didn't point out that she was a woman and he didn't mutter "bitch" aloud, even if she could hear it anyway. Oddly, that's how she'd gotten her tag, she'd threatened to kill the next bastard who called her a bitch. It was Day Two of the month-long Delta Force Operator Selection. "Killer Kristine" had sounded from a Green Beret wag...and it had stuck. As had she. The Green Beret hadn't made it to Week Two—not her doing either.

Besides, the name was far too appropriate, even if no one would ever know. She let it stick because it was God's honest truth.

Cursing herself before she even did it, she tied another MOLLE harness onto her pack along with a dozen empty utility pouches threaded into the straps. Whatever the good Dr. Ray Ewing felt he needed to take out of the country, he could damn well carry it in his own rig.

"Ready, Mankowski?"

"Gotta pee."

"You've got until I reach the helo, then we're leaving you behind."

"Sure, Killer." But then he looked at her face and hurried toward the can.

Yeah, "Bitch" versus "Killer." Everyone meant it the same way. Thank God that Delta Force favored individual capabilities over team capabilities or she'd be out on her ass. Delta operators worked in solo or pairs and only came together when they had to. SEALs, however, hated breaking into smaller teams even *when* they had to—it tended to make them snivel like sad puppy dogs.

She did take the steps from the Hangar Deck up to the flight deck slowly, so the Black Hawk was just easing off its wheels when Girlie Mankowski dove through the cargo door.

"What's wrong with you, man?" He was seriously ticked, probably about the long, wet dribble down his pantleg where he'd pulled it in before he was quite done.

She knew only too damned well what was wrong with her.

3

"Five klicks back out," Mankowski whined.

The sea had been kicking up rough and their small Zodiac boat had made hard work of reaching the coast from where the Night Stalkers had dropped them. They'd made it, but a glance at the charge on the batteries said there was no way the electric motor was getting them back to the pickup point.

"We'll find some other transport. Sink it."

Mankowski groaned, but did as she instructed. She felt battered as well, but the weather was picking up and it would an even harder ride back out. No way his doctoral eminence would make it in a rubber boat even if they had the power.

With the charges set, Mankowski aimed the tiny boat out of the inner La Guaira harbor. They'd landed near the entry of the long harbor formed by a massive two-kilometer-long breakwater that arced outward and then paralleled the Venezuelan coast, creating a narrow line of protected wharves. The autopilot held the little boat in line out into the darkness, plunging over the waves that had so inundated them on the trip in.

The Zodiac made it three hundred meters out before the charges fired. Even with night-vision goggles it was hard to see the flashes that ruptured all of the bladders and destroyed the motor as well. Already unidentifiable, in seconds it would be at the bottom of the Atlantic.

"Now what?"

Kristine surveyed the long breakwater of heavy granite stone as another wave shattered on its far side and sent spray climbing skyward. She wasn't going to complain about having a bigger boat when they ventured back to sea. Even if it was physically impossible to get any wetter after their night crossing, she could feel her gear becoming heavier by the second with water weight. Especially all of the extra kit for *himself.* No one had bothered to tell lowly Delta operators why he was so damned important.

"Go find us a boat."

"*What?*"

"This harbor has commercial, ferry, and naval piers. I can see a half-dozen boats from here. Night Stalkers will be on station in five hours to retrieve us. You have four hours to find one and pick us up right here. But don't grab it until I radio that I've got him and we're coming out." She always did better on her own anyway.

Mankowski didn't look happy, but he didn't argue.

They went their separate ways. Him scouting the two kilometers of wharves to the southeast while, moving quickly over the big stones that lined the public ferry terminal; her making her way west.

Just as planned, she ducked out of the passenger terminal, closed for the night, and slipped through the fence into the yard for the goods shipping terminal. What the satellite photos hadn't really showed was just how few container ships were willing to deliver goods to a country that could no longer pay any of its bills. Some of the largest crude reserves in the world and they were bankrupt. Beyond bankrupt, the people were starving to death before they could die of poor health care, broken sanitation, and all the other disasters here that made Brooklyn, New York look almost habitable.

She'd planned on dodging through the container field...except there were far more open spaces than containers in the yard. That wasn't at all helpful.

While she was surveying her options, one of the country's notorious blackouts conveniently rolled through. Taking the risk, she sprinted across a long open stretch. The power and lights didn't come back on until she was out of the yard, across the street, and through the electric fence that was supposed to be protecting Naval Base Antonio Picardi. She even had time to resplice the section she'd cut so that no one would know she'd crossed through. It would also make it that much faster when she crossed back out.

Inside the base, she lay under some leaves of a *palma llanera* that the wind was beating into a frenzy loud enough that she couldn't hear herself think. The storm was really kicking some unpredicted ass, which would make for better cover and made her happier that the Zodiac was at the bottom of the Atlantic.

Straight ahead lay an Olympic-sized swimming pool

with diving boards, lounge chairs, folded up and now flopped over umbrellas, and a serious-looking bar and food stand, currently well-shuttered. It was almost midnight, so that made sense.

It was a good thing that the general populace wasn't starving to death or anything. Oh, wait, they were. Just the military wasn't. No wonder the assholes were loyal— they had the only cushy jobs left in the country.

At that moment, a surprisingly cold rain slashed out of the darkness.

Yep! It was a Delta-style fun night.

4

THANKFULLY, THE BOLIVARIAN NAVY OF VENEZUELA FELT themselves to be sacrosanct. In the midst of the storm, there were very few patrols and none with night-vision gear or much interest in anything other than getting back under cover after hurrying along their prescribed routes.

In an hour she'd worked around a dormitory, mess hall, and training center—probably could have done it in half the time with how lame the patrols were. The sheeting rain didn't let up and they were doing their duty on the hustle with their heads down.

Ultimately, Building Fourteen was right where the spy for the opposition had said it would be; not all of the military loved their corrupt, paranoid president-turned-dictator-turned-total bastard. The mole had given the CIA the tip about where to find Dr. Ewing—in the secure detention facility on the third floor.

Apparently the CIA had gotten tired of waiting for the government to finally collapse under its own weight. In her estimation that wasn't the issue. The real issue was that if the military and the SEBIN secret police finally went down hard, they sure weren't going to leave behind any prisoners to tell the tale. Either way, tonight was Ewing's lucky night.

Kristine waited for the latest patrol to sweep by. Figuring that the most secure position was close behind them, she hurried along in their wake, circling Building Fourteen. As she went, she strategically placed charges she might need to make good their escape.

The moment the patrol ducked inside, she stepped out into the courtyard and gauged the height of the building—three stories, nine to ten meters. Reaching back over her left shoulder, she snagged the lifting loop on her grappling hook and pulled it and a hank of 9mm tactical line free from its PALS pouch. With a practiced flick of her wrist, she spread the three tines out and they clicked into place.

Five fast spins and she had smooth control of the spinning grapple. With a hard upward release, it soared aloft in a high arc. The coil of tactical line slid off her palm in a neat flow. For a moment she thought a gust of wind was going to ruin her throw, but an immediate counter gust dropped it well over the roof's edge. A sharp tug gave her under a meter of slippage and then a hard set that easily took her weight.

She snapped a pair of hand jumars onto the line, walked her feet up onto the wall, and began working the ascenders. They slid upward without resistance, but not downward unless she hit the release. Two minutes later, she lay on the roof pulling up the line.

The wind, which had been blocked while she was

down among the buildings, whipped hard at her. Much more and they'd be in a tropical storm. Wouldn't that be a joy.

A quick tour of the roof revealed the maintenance hatch. Locked from the inside, she snapped together a thermite torch—about the size of a three-D-cell flashlight —put on dark glasses, and cut the hinges off. Five thousand degrees of fun. There were some things she loved about Delta Force, and the cool toys factor was definitely high on the list.

She dropped into the middle of Building Fourteen's detention floor. Nightlights illuminated the corridor and a guard sleeping at the far end of it. Make that drunk and asleep because her entry letting in the storm had been far from silent. She woke him up with a strip of duct tape over his mouth, then cuffed him to his heavy chair with zip ties.

"Which cell is Dr. Ewing in?" Kristine whispered in Spanish as she pressed the tip of the torch under his chin. She'd let him see it just enough to know that it was like nothing he'd ever seen before, not that she was planning to melt open his head with it. "Grunt the number of times for his number."

The guy's eyes rolled in panic.

"Now or I'll tape over your nose too and leave you to rot."

Apparently he believed her and grunted out a six.

5

———

CELL SIX WAS THIRD ON THE LEFT. THROUGH THE observation window she couldn't see shit. Flipping down her night-vision goggles, she could see that it was a much larger space than she'd anticipated. A man lay asleep on a corner cot. To the other side was a long workbench with a computer and an array of stuff that looked like a chemist's lab.

She hit the light switch—which was on her side of the door—and shoved her goggles back up.

The guy on the couch rolled over and blinked his eyes hard. The face matched the briefing and she unlocked the door.

"Who?" He grunted out in Spanish, then blinked harder as he focused on her. "You don't look like the other military. I mean aside from being female."

"I'm not. I don't fit in even among female military." She dropped her pack and peeled off the IOTV body armor. She suddenly felt thirty pounds lighter. "Put this on. We're on the move."

"To where?"

"What do you care?" Then she cursed herself. He probably did. "The US, if we don't screw this up."

"Rockin'!" Not quite the staid scientist she'd been expecting. In fact, he sounded New York. And he was somewhere around her age, another detail the briefing docs hadn't included.

As she helped him into the gear, and ignored his embarrassed grunt of surprise—civilians were so fussy— as she reached between his legs to pull through the strap connecting the butt- to the groin-protectors. "You'll need this MOLLE as well." She freed it from her pack and dumped the vest over his head.

"A vest named Molly?" Ewing switched to English.

"M.O.L.L.E. Modular Lightweight Load-carrying Equipment. The pouches are for whatever you want to take from here."

"Well, that would have a silent E, not a Y sound," he continued as he moved about the room and began stuffing various items into his pockets. It looked almost random, but he didn't strike her as a random sort of guy. Still, it was an odd selection: various sealed flasks, some baggies of assorted powders, and a very dog-eared novel. "Haven't finished it yet," as he tore off the first two-thirds before she could see what it was and stuffed the last third in a plastic bag and then into a pouch. Marks for efficiency, cross off absent-minded. "English doesn't have that sound Y for a final E. If we go back to the Spanish, you would get mol-lay, like the Mexican chocolate sauce with an extra L. Still not Molly."

"Do you want to talk pronunciation all day or can we get your ass out of here?"

He stopped and glanced around the room, looking at last at the chemist's bench. "If I never have to calculate another mole of cocaine or manufacture another mole of scopolamine (which doesn't work as a truth serum no matter what the SEBIN thinks), I'll die a happy man."

"A mole?"

"Not the small one on your right cheek—which looks good on you by the way—nor the brown furry animal, though a mole of cocaine actually weighs about three brown-furry moles, a third of a kilo. I like that as a unit of measure. A mole, not the brown-furry one but the chemical one, is a six followed by twenty-three zeroes' worth of atoms. It's not actually a weight, but rather a quantity. Because it's such a simpler atom, a mole of pure carbon-12 weighs over twenty-five times less than a mole of cocaine or about point-oh-eight of a brown-furry."

"That's a bunch of atoms," she couldn't help saying. No way was she getting into a conversation about brown-furries, their mass or otherwise. And she already knew men thought she was attractive, which was way more trouble than it was worth.

"A mole, the chemical one, is about six hundred times more atoms than there are stars in the known universe. Atoms are seriously small buggers. Why are we still standing here talking about this?"

There was something about the way he talked that kept her listening. Kristine had to physically shake herself to break the mild hypnosis.

Back out in the hall, she wasn't even halfway back to

the maintenance hatch when Ewing called out. "What about all of them?" He was looking at the closed cell doors.

"There's no way I can extract them with you. If I release them all, they'd just be recaptured or gunned down."

"If they're in their cells, they don't stand a chance at all. Give me the keys."

"We don't have time for this."

Dr. Ray Ewing drew himself up to his full height— about an inch over her own five-eight—and did his best to stare down at her haughtily. The effect was also ruined by how gaunt he was. She was a little surprised that he was still upright beneath the weight of the IOTV's armor plates and everything else he'd been through. But there was no doubting his grimly determined eyes. He'd face down the Devil herself to give his fellow prisoners a chance.

Feeling small in a way she didn't appreciate, she tossed him the keys.

He unlocked the first door, then the second.

"We don't have time for this." But he ignored her mutter.

Ewing walked up to the first prisoner to stagger out into the open. "Here are the keys. Unlock every door before you leave. Every single one, *si?*" The man glanced down the hall at the muzzled guard, then nodded fiercely before snatching away the keys and moving to the next door as fast as his feet could carry him.

"They still don't have a chance, but I feel better about it."

Kristine inspected him and liked what she saw. Liked it a lot. "Do you know how to shoot a gun?"

He shook his head no.

"Good!"

That earned her a confused laugh.

She fished out the spare she'd brought for him just in case he did, and after a moment's debate, her ankle piece as well.

"Who here knows how to shoot?" she asked the prisoners gathering in the narrow hallway. Three came forward. She handed over her two weapons with extra magazines and sent the third person to where she'd kicked aside the guard's rifle. Then she pulled out an explosive's digital timer, without the explosive attached, and set it for three minutes. Starting it, she set her own watch to match a three-minute countdown.

"You," she reached out and grabbed the first unarmed man who came to hand. "Do not let anyone leave this floor until this counter hits zero. At that time, the guards below will think there is an attack all along the north and east side. If you wait for that, then rush out of the building to the southwest, you'll stand a chance. *Comprende?*"

"*Si, bonita señorita. Si! Si! Gracias! Cero segundos,*" he held the timer with both hands like it was precious.

6
———

THIS TIME, EWING CAME WHEN SHE DRAGGED HIM DOWN the corridor to the maintenance hatch ladder. He gasped in surprise as he crawled out the hatch into the battering rain and wind. *And here comes the whining...*

"I forgot what fresh air tastes like."

"It tastes wet."

His laugh was encouraging, but he didn't look strong enough to control his own descent. She tied the end of her grapple rope to his MOLLE vest's lifting ring and took a bight of rope about her waist before guiding him over the roof's edge.

"Don't drop me," he pleaded as he eased over the lip.

"Well," she grunted as she took his weight, "you weigh a lot more than a brown-furry. More like a mole of brown-furries, but I'll try not to."

"No, that would be roughly two to the twentieth tons and that's—" she lowered him out of sight and let the wind snatch the math right out of his mouth.

By the time he was down, she was running short on

time. Kristine took a loop in between her feet and hand-over-handed her way down. On the ground, she grabbed Ewing's hand so that she could gauge his capabilities and sprinted away. In another twenty-eight seconds the Venezuelan Navy was going to have something far bigger than a mysterious rope to worry about.

They rushed out past the corner of the mess hall and the dorm. He didn't stumble often, though he tended to slide around on the muddy ground. She could also feel him lagging even after a twenty-second sprint—she'd have to account for that.

Her watch hit zero just as they ducked out of sight beneath the marginal shelter of a yellow ipê tree. She hoped the freed prisoners hadn't jumped the gun. Pulling out her remote detonator, she selected all the charges she'd set to the north and east, then hit their firing transmitters simultaneously.

The whole corner of Building Fourteen seemed to explode.

"Holy shit!" Ewing cried out.

"Quiet, unless you want a patrol coming up our asses."

"You blew up the building with those poor people still in it. What kind of person are you?" He sounded seriously pissed, but at least he was a little quieter about it.

"I'm Killer Kristine. But try looking again." She needed to be in motion, but she wouldn't mind at least one person in this screwed up world thinking well of her.

Every door and most of the windows had been shattered, but she'd only used breaching charges. A flash and hard bang; most of the energy had been directed into destroying the doors themselves.

"Here," she unclipped her night-vision googles and held them out before pointing off to the west. By the fire's light, she could see the stream of prisoners departing the building in the other direction. The patrols and guards stumbled forward to stare into the firelight to the northeast like so many pigeons. It was very tempting to unsling her rifle and start picking them off, but that would draw the kind of attention she didn't want.

"They're getting away," Ewing sounded so pleased.

"We'll see." Their chances still weren't great, but at least they were free for now. "About time we were doing some of that ourselves."

7

———

Clear of the Naval base, out through the bypasses she'd set in the electric fence, they were resting between a pair of containers in the shipping yard that blocked the worst of the slashing rain.

"Do you have any food?"

She should have thought of that, and dug out a pair of MREs from her pack. "Pick one."

"What's the difference?"

She shrugged. "Twenty-four so-called menus; these are two of them. Once you get rid of all the extra wrappings, heaters, and candy, they're all pretty much the same."

"Why do you get rid of the candy?" He took one and began futilely tugging at one corner.

Snapping down with her wrist, her Infidel blade dropped into her palm. Hitting the release, the anodized four-inch double-edged dagger snapped out of the front of the handle.

Ewing dropped his MRE pouches in surprise. *Civilian.*

"Candy is bad luck. Never eat it on a mission." She slit open his pouches then peeked in. "You've got the Mexican Chicken. Not a bad menu, though not great cold." She slit her own. "I've got Spaghetti in Beef Sauce if you'd prefer."

"Cold spaghetti versus cold Mexican chicken. You really live the highlife. Why 'Killer Kristine'? I haven't seen you kill a single person yet."

"I was in a good mood."

"Happen much?" He dug into his pouch with a spork and began eating fast. Most civilians weren't fans of MREs, but he ate it like it was some fancy-kind-of-place good.

"That I have to kill people or that I'm in a good mood?"

"We'll start with the former," he'd finished the chicken, fruit pack, cheddar cheese-filled pretzels, and chocolate bar (which didn't count as candy so it was safe). She slit open and handed over her untouched meal and he started in on that.

Reluctant to answer, she stared up and blinked into the spattering rain that found its way between the shipping containers. *Sure! I've killed all sorts. Psychotic ragheads at two paces and hell-bent Congolese warlords at a thousand. I've taken out narco-runners in Honduras and nacro-manufacturers in Colombia.* Civilians didn't react well to hearing about such things and she'd learned to keep them to herself. *So, you're a killer for the Army?* Rather than taking them down, she'd just say, *I'm a soldier for the same government that builds your bridges and keeps your food safe.* It never seemed to work. Safer to keep her mouth shut.

"I'll take that as a yes," Ewing said between bites of his Chocolate Chip Toaster Pastry and Italian Bread Sticks.

She shrugged. "And?" Kristine waited for whatever weird reaction was coming her way. She wasn't real hungry and didn't bother fishing out another menu.

"Not what you'd expect from a beautiful woman. That's all. Of course, first impressions don't lie, I suppose. You looked amazingly good standing there in my door all kitted up for war. I was down here doing research for their oil fields. Then they showed up one day and I became a government slave instead."

"You mean until you got caught as a spy for the CIA?"

He inspected her carefully.

"It's the only thing that fits. I've worked enough CIA special requests to know the feel of them."

"What are you?"

"You asked that before."

"You said Killer Kristine. But that's when I asked what kind of a person you were."

"I'm Delta Force. Pleased ta meetcha."

"Brooklyn! What part?"

She'd worked hard to knock it out of her voice over the years, but it had slipped out in the old pat phrase. "Along the Gowanus."

"Which side?"

"You know the good parts? Nowhere near those."

He actually laughed. "Didn't know the Gowanus had good parts."

Ewing was right, of course. The mile-long canal in the heart of Brooklyn was still one of the most polluted stretches of water in the entire country. It was a Superfund cleanup site, except no one could figure out how to clean up three centuries of toxic sludge without digging up a whole section of Brooklyn and burying it somewhere that no one cared about, like Queens.

"It *doesn't* have any good parts," as Kristine well knew. "But we lived in the part that killed my little sister when she went swimming in it one day."

"Oh God! I'm so sorry." And Ewing simply reached a hand around her shoulder in a sideways hug.

Something cracked inside her like the lightning bolt of the growing storm that briefly revealed a flash of his concerned face.

"I was supposed to take her out for an ice cream; it was so hot. Ran into some of my friends and forgot to keep an eye on her. She got bored and went swimming. Even dove down for something shiny in the mud. The toxins took her out in under a month."

And never once since had Kristine told anyone about it. Never told a soul how her family had disavowed her. How she did her best to never use her last name unless she had to in order to avoid hurting the family—another reason to not fight back against Killer Kristine. Now, here she sat with a total stranger in a raging storm in Venezuela, spilling her guts.

How the hell had that happened?

But Ewing's arm around her shoulder felt good. Despite all the gear they both wore and all the pain snarled in her gut.

It felt good.

"I grew up on Carroll Street, just a few blocks up from the canal," he whispered barely louder than the wind shrieking by overhead. "That's how I became a chemist. Trying to figure out how to fix that canal."

"Can you?" The flash of hope hurt almost as much as the cold memory. She'd joined the Army the day of her sister's funeral—a funeral at which not a soul had sat with her or spoken to her.

"Not yet, sorry. But I still work on it when I can. That's what I brought from the cell," he patted the pouches on his MOLLE. "Whenever I could find time, I'd work on finding a reagent that might fix some aspect of the mess without killing everyone who lives near it."

She didn't know whether to be sick that there was still nothing that could save others like her sister or feel overwhelming hope that people were still trying. "Are you a good chemist?"

"Good enough that the CIA recruited me and the Venezuelan's didn't kill me when they found out." He offered the first real hope she'd felt in a long time.

She yanked out her radio. "Gotta get your ass out of here."

8

Mankowski had answered right away. "I've got a beauty staked out. Just say go and I'll be there in ten."

"Go!" Then she'd gotten Dr. Ray Ewing on the move. She now had another reason to keep him alive, a far more important one than she'd started the night with.

Again, she took his hand to keep exact tabs on him. It felt like more than that, but...something best ignored. Together, they slipped up to the end of the container alley and surveyed the surroundings. Not a soul in sight and even though the yard lights were back on, the visibility sucked beyond about twenty meters. Good.

It took them eight of the ten minutes to scoot across the shipping yard and back to the ferry terminal where she'd left Mankowski.

"We're good here," she got Ray tucked out of sight between some big boulders and a support stanchion for the ferry dock overhead that did impressively little to block the slashing storm. "We just— Oh shit!"

"What?"

She slapped her silenced sidearm into his hands. "It's loaded. There's no safety. Just aim and pull the trigger. Try not to shoot either of us in the process." Kristine unslung her HK416, powered up the night sights, and zeroed in on the approaching patrol boat.

It should be out in the middle of the channel right now.

On a foul night like tonight, it should be tied up at the pier.

It definitely shouldn't be gliding straight toward her position at the ferry landing.

The lights in the ferry terminal above them were off for the night, but there was enough splash from the commercial yard that Kristine knew she wouldn't be invisible much longer.

Only person that she could see was standing at the helm inside the high, glassed-in bridge of the seventy-five foot long patrol boat. The boat was light blue, with PG-401 painted on either side of the bow. A Gavión-class patrol boat built in the US decades ago, with fore and aft swivel-mounted machine guns. Except there was no one manning the guns.

She zeroed in on the helmsman who was...waving.

9
——————

"Can't believe you know how to drive this thing. I'm so totally renaming you, Connie 'Boatman' Mankowski."

"Why thanks, Killer Kristine," he grinned as he backed them away from the ferry dock. "Beats the shit out of Girlie. Never could seem to shed that one. Did some time as a yacht crew off Martha's Vineyard. Pilot gave me lessons when we were running the boat empty to fetch the owners somewhere or other."

"Maybe it's time you shed Killer, Kristine," Ray said softly from close beside her, too softly for Boatman to hear.

Boatman nosed them toward the end of the breakwater, almost invisible in the spray now breaking over it.

She could only shake her head. "I'll take rear gun until we're clear. Stay in here where it's dry, Ray. It's still dumping out there."

"Ooo, never heard the Captain call any man by his first name. Look out, buddy. She's gunning for you."

Kristine considered beating the shit out of Boatman where he stood at the wheel. Not a good choice as she'd never driven anything bigger than the sunken Zodiac. She could figure it out if she had to but it wouldn't be pretty, especially not in a storm.

The wind tore at her as she stepped out the door and hung onto the rail heading aft.

"That's a mole, too." Ray... No, Ewing...no...Ray—she sighed to herself—followed her out onto the deck.

"What is? No brown-furries. No stars with twenty-one zeroes after the one—you said there was six hundred times less stars than atoms in a mole." She slogged down the three steps to the rear recovery deck, around the launch cradled there, and stepped up to the rear gun. A .50 cal M2 Browning deck gun. Sweet! Nobody had better mess with her tonight.

"Women who know math are very sexy. You realize that?"

"Soldier doesn't equal stupid," she did her best to ignore his comment. Though it might be the first time a man had called her that while not talking about her body.

"Mole, noun," he announced in a professorial tone. "A long pier or breakwater of piled rock. Actually, you get two for one, because a mole is also the harbor protected by a mole. Like a mole squared."

"A thirty-six with forty-six zeroes after it. Or do you prefer a three-point-six with forty-seven zeroes?"

"Very sexy," he whispered just a tone above another gust of wind that slashed salt water in their faces. "A mole of moles being discussed in a mole-harbor protected by a mole-breakwater," Ray sounded very pleased. "Spoken by a smart and lovely soldier lady with a mole on her cheek, who a mole-spy tipped off to my whereabouts—and I now have a belly full of mole sauce—and she's still wearing her MOLLE harness which—"

"I think we've beat that joke to death now, even if you can figure out how to work brown-furries into that sentence." She snapped safety lines from the boat to their MOLLEs and braced herself. The first storm waves were slipping around the corner of Ray's breakwater-mole and slamming into the boat. There didn't appear to be any unwanted attention due to their departure. If anyone on shore did notice, they weren't doing anything about it that she could see. Not that anyone else was dumb enough to be out in this filthy weather.

"You know you aren't responsible for her death," Ray went suddenly serious.

Kristine could only grunt at the stab that had just bypassed all of her lifetime's defenses.

"You didn't kill your sister," he declared as if he knew what the fuck he was talking about.

"*So* did!"

"No," his voice stayed dead calm. "There's a reason that the word 'accident' occurs in the English language. Have you been blaming yourself for that for your whole life?"

The lights of the inner harbor were falling behind them as the patrol boat lifted its bow into the first big wave.

"I killed her as surely as if I held the gun to her head myself."

"Did you? Goddamn it, Kristine!" Ray yanked on the shoulder strap of her MOLLE to spin her to face him. He practically shook her by it though she was definitely the stronger one. "No wonder they call you Killer. You've been killing your own soul with that load for how long?"

"My entire life since." She could taste the tears coming down her cheeks despite the sea salt spray. She hadn't cried since...since that day.

"Get a clue woman. You made yourself a Delta Force captain. And you just saved my life and the lives of how many others pretty much single-handed. Go ahead, tell me how many women could pull that off. Oh wait, let me guess: one? Maybe two? Gotta rename you Kristine the Incredible or something."

The first big surf slammed against them. She kept them anchored with one hand on the gun. They each had a hand on the other's MOLLE and the wave's force slammed them together.

While the wave disappeared behind them and the patrol boat climbed the next big one, they didn't ease back. Instead, she pulled him the last inch closer.

Maybe Dr. Ray Ewing was right and it was time to drop that load astern.

She kissed him hard as the next big wave rolled by beneath them and lifted them up.

Yes, she definitely needed a new name. And maybe, just maybe, one was finally coming her way.

DELTA MISSION: OPERATION RUDOLPH

*In three days, **Betsy** retires from a decade as a Delta Force tracker and shooter. But a training mission gone wrong...or perhaps "strange" is a better word...sets her one last challenge.*

*St. Nick's lead reindeer, whose name is actually Jeremy, has gone missing. The dangerously handsome **Chief Herder Elf Horatio,** needs the best tracker in any world.*

Is Betsy hallucinating?

Can Christmas be saved?

Is there enough time left for: Delta Mission: Operation Rudolph?

INTRODUCTION

It's fun to end on a silly note.

I so enjoy writing my Christmas romance stories. Sometimes they're serious, other times fun, but I'd never written one that was flat-out silly.

And I figured that if I was going for silly, I needed someone who was decidedly not silly.

That was easy...Delta Force.

Range 37, in addition to being the setting for the sniper trials for Cindy Sue in *Love in the Drop Zone* above, also has an urban battle zone, room-clearing mazes, and more. So I had my starting point.

Then I had the influence of three different books.

Chuck Pfarrer's memoir of his years as a Navy SEAL, *Warrior Soul,* gave me my opening. He recounts that even though it was his last full day in the service, the schedule had said he was due for a dangerous training mission, so, of course, he did the training...and was nearly killed the day before he retired.

Perfect. My heroine Betsy is retiring after today,

except she has one more training to do, which goes strangely wrong.

This is where two other stories came to my aid. They demonstrate how we can reinterpret something, and make it completely our own.

J. R. R. Tolkien wrote a series of Christmas letters to his nieces and nephews during World War II. They were hand-illustrated and were filled with the latest news from the North Pole. They told of the daily lives of Santa, the elves, a particularly foolish polar bear, gnome invasions, and all of the other challenges that delivering presents around the world entails.

I reached into his collection strictly for the sense of silly.

And from Jan Brett's lovely *The Wild Christmas Reindeer* I took the idea of Santa's chief reindeer herder having trouble.

Ardent fans will find connections between Jeremy, Santa's lead reindeer, and Henderson's Ranch #5, *Big Sky, Loyal Heart* during Lauren's hunting expedition.

It's a wonderful, silly romp.

That it also looks at a Delta Force operator's tenacity, adaptability, and skill at wilderness tracking is completely beside the point.

1
———

Live-fire training.

She didn't need any blasted live-fire training. Especially not during a freak snowstorm that was inundating Range 37 at Fort Bragg, North Carolina. Betsy's personal thermostat was currently set to Congo jungle, not three-days-before-Christmas blizzard.

Okay, the pretty white flakes fluttering down on the rifle range didn't count as a blizzard—though she'd grown up in Arkansas and it was more than she was used to—but it was cold enough that they were sticking to everything, including her. And her breath showed in puffs. She focused on breathing only through her nose to cut down on the clouds that might give away her position to the instructors.

The fact that she was out of Delta Force and the Army in three more days didn't matter to them. She'd done her decade in the field and Christmas Day would mark her release from service. But when command said you did a training, you did one. She was theirs to order about until the moment she walked out the gate.

Betsy kept low behind a stone wall and pondered the enemy's next move. She'd barely had a glimpse of the artificial town that was the core of the training range's purpose. The Fort Bragg training squadron was always rearranging it in unexpected ways. She'd been in the field for a full year on her latest deployment, so the hundreds of hours she'd spent here over the years were now irrelevant.

The hundred-plus acres of Range 37 was a 360-degree, live-fire shoothouse. Some parts were modern urban, others Kandahar Province-low-and-crammed-together.

What kind of idiot training scenario sent a solo soldier on a snatch-and-grab mission? Minimum for that type of operation was a four-man team: two to grab, two to guard. Instead, they'd sent her in on her own without any explanation.

The only way out is through. Old axiom.

Of course solo was the story of her life. Dad gone from the beginning. While her high school classmates had been discovering friends and sex, she'd been caring for her mother through a fatal bout of cancer. Delta Force, the true loners of the US military, had been as natural to her as breathing. One of the only women there? Sure. Whatever.

But a one-woman snatch-and-grab operation? She was probably the best they had for that—no matter how stupid an idea it was. Perhaps they were using her to test some crazy scenario just to see how it worked.

Fine! Time to show them just what she *could* do.

She lay down in the snow and fast-rolled across the gap between the stone wall she'd been crouched behind and the brick building next over. As she rolled, she kept her rifle scope to her eye. Her best moving shot for rooftops was actually on her back, not her stomach—an unlikely trick she'd learned by accident in Mosul. Head tipped back, HK416 at the ready, she spotted two hostiles atop the wall on the far side of a broad courtyard. She hit both from her back, rolled onto her stomach, double-tapped an armed bad guy target crouching by a plywood maple tree, then two more into the mannequins on the roof from her back just to make sure the targets stayed dead.

The six hard clangs of bullets striking metal targets registered only after she was safe behind the red brick.

She held her fire as two children mannequins peeked at her from a nearby window. A dummy woman rushed across the street, her form gliding on a hidden track. A rough-painted man close behind her, using the woman figure as a shield, had an AK-47. The harsh ring of metal echoed between the buildings as Betsy shot him in the knee through the fluttering back of the woman's dress— then twice in the face as soon the mannequin shifted aside.

As she rolled around the end of the wall, and dove for fresh cover, a particularly large snowflake plastered itself across the lens of her shooting goggles. It left a wet smear when she brushed it aside.

Betsy had tracked her quarry off the edge of the map somewhere, slipping out of simulated Afghanistan into a quaint French village setting that she didn't recall ever seeing before.

The next building over, probably just painted plywood, was an exceptional imitation of rose-and-gray stonework, medieval arches, and cobbled streets barely wide enough for two donkeys to pass. It would make a resting place for the Merovingian French kings back before the Dark Ages. With the snow, it looked perfect for finding a little Provençal bistro with a mug of mulled wine and a cozy chair by a stone fireplace.

Of course the best that would be waiting for her after this would be a hot cup of coffee and a burger at the SWCS DFAC—the Special Warfare Center and School Dining Facility. If she didn't freeze to death first.

A glance back the way she'd come to make sure no one was behind her and—

Betsy blinked hard, as if that would clear away the obscuring snow.

There was no longer an Afghan town behind her, though she knew she'd just been through one. She was at the center of a French village that looked too authentic, even for Range 37. Alleys twisted. Yew trees, so old and gnarled they truly might have been planted by some ancient French king, rose before a two-story, stone, row house. A cluster of dormant rose vines climbed a nearby wall, some of the stems thicker than her arm. They'd been there a while...a long while.

An actual donkey, pulling a tiny cart bearing a large wine barrel, clopped along, his unshod hooves muffled by the fallen snow. The hard rattle of the two ironclad, wooden wheels sounded from the cobbles.

She spun back to look down the street where she'd just shot the target with an AK-47. More people flowed across the courtyard now, but not gliding on any hidden rail. Some carried gigantic woven baskets, others wooden platters of food—all hurrying this way and that as if preparing for some event. Their clothing was loose and broadcloth.

And puffs of breath were coming out of their mouths.

There weren't supposed to be any real people in a live-fire training except the attackers—in this scenario, just her. If she made a mistake, she could kill an innocent, not that she ever had. She'd always scored perfect marks in target discernment on the range and in the field. A man came out a doorway close beside where she lay in the snow and almost stepped on her.

"Excusez-moi." He definitely spoke before hurrying down the road. Not a mannequin.

She sat up carefully, keeping her eye out for potential shooters. All of the people on the streets—and there were more with each passing moment—were dressed for some form of medieval village reenactment like the Norwegian Folk Museum in Oslo, only more French-Grand-Master-painting-come-to-life than simplistic-Nordic.

Not a one looked at her. She glanced down at herself to be sure that she hadn't changed as well. Army boots, camo pants, Kevlar shooter's vest filled with spare magazines for her rifle and a Glock still in its holster. She indeed still held her HK416 rifle and could feel the helmet on her head. Another blink, and she could feel her eyelashes brushing on the inside of her shooter goggles.

"What the hell?"

Even the air smelled different. Baked breads, wood fires, roasting meat that made her stomach growl.

Only one man was out of place now. He stood in the exact center of the courtyard and was looking directly at her.

Out of place! The alarm went off in her head. Instinct kicked in and she aimed and fired, only at the last moment realizing that he held no weapon. She tried to shift her aim, but knew it wasn't enough.

The man leaned slightly to one side and the bullet missed his cheek by a hair's breadth, smacking into a stone arch behind him and releasing a puff of rock dust as it pulverized itself.

Then, as calm as could be, he looked back at her.

Nobody, but nobody dodged a round fired from an HK416.

2

BETSY COULD ONLY STARE AT HIM AS THE VILLAGERS continued to mill about without paying any attention to either of them. By now the donkey had drawn even with her position. She reached out to touch it. Though she wore thin gloves, it felt real enough.

The man, however, didn't look real. Six feet tall, but slender as a willow branch. He didn't look unfit or misproportioned, just impossibly slender. He had glorious black hair that fell to his waist, whereas her own blonde was short-cropped and barely reached her jawline. He had a long face with high cheekbones, pale skin, and the bluest eyes she'd ever seen. He was dressed in form-fitting black leather that might be appropriate for a chick on a motorcycle calendar. It did look very fine on him, so maybe she finally understood why guys went so ape over those kinds of calendars. A little. Not much really.

One thing was for certain, though. It made him look even more out of place in Medieval France than she did.

She couldn't react, couldn't find it in her to move as he stepped among the hurrying townsfolk until he was standing just an arm's-length away. A thin red line scored his cheek.

He noticed the direction of her attention and raised a hand to brush at it.

"I'll have to remember to move faster in future encounters."

"Move. Faster." People didn't step aside from bullets moving at 890 meters per second.

His smile was brief, but dazzling and she could only blink in surprise.

"But…" She didn't know "but" what, but it was the only sound she could make.

"I'm Horatio."

"Horatio?"

"Yes," his voice was impossibly deep and sounded more like flowing water than spoken words.

"Is that like 'Go West, Young Man' Horatio Alger? Or 'Alas, poor Yorick' in Hamlet?"

"Nor Captain Horatio Hornblower. Just Horatio the Herder."

"The herder of what? Who…" No. "*What* are you?" She forced herself to look away from his dazzling blue eyes. Her gaze landed on a prominently pointed ear where the chill wind blew aside an elegant length of his hair like some runway model's. He was both the handsomest and the prettiest man she'd ever seen, even if he wasn't one.

A group of children, ones she'd have labeled as beggars, gathered together in a group and began to sing in Latin. As a child, she'd chosen to do her confirmation into the Roman Catholic church in Latin. As an adult, she could only wonder why she'd bothered with any of it.

Orientis partibus
adventavit asinus,
pulcher et fortissimus,
Sarcinis aptissimus.

"From the east, the pretty Advent donkey carries the sacred baggage?" Maybe not so much with her Catholic school Latin.

"It is an ancient Latin Christmas carol, popular in twelfth-century France," the man waved his long-fingered hand negligently about as if that was somehow where they were. "In your language it is called *The Friendly Beasts* and relates the legend of the animals who helped with the birth of Jesus. That verse is the donkey telling of carrying Mary to the manger."

"Oh." What else was she supposed to say to such a crazy statement. She considered for a moment. This *definitely* wasn't Range 37. She rose to her toes and tried clicking the heels of her Army boots together three times.

Nothing changed.

Maybe it only worked for ruby Army boots.

Horatio smiled at her as if he knew exactly what she was doing.

"Allow me to escort you elsewhere," he turned sideways to her and offered his arm. At a loss for what else to do, she shifted her rifle to her other hand—in shooting, all Delta operators were ambidextrous— left the safety off, and slipped her fingers about his elbow. He felt as thin as he looked, but he felt as strong as a seasoned operator who could hike fifty kilometers with a full pack, just to get *into* battle.

He led her down the street to a doorway that had a wooden sign hung above it depicting a cluster of grapes, and led her inside. The smoke from the big, ill-vented, stone fireplace stung her eyes and there was a rank smell like an entire Delta platoon that had been in the field for a month without bathing. But beneath that, the cinnamon and nutmeg of mulled wine and the richness of mutton stew filled the air.

Horatio sat with the elegance of a powerful man at a small, rough table close by the warm fire. She propped her rifle against the wall close to hand and sat across from him. Their knees brushed together comfortably. He didn't draw away, but neither did he press. It was merely comfortable, friendly even. Not something she was used to with men. For the most part they either wanted sex or wanted her to get the hell out of the boys' club military unit. Horatio the Herder was harder to read and she rather liked that bit of mystery.

In moments, they were served with clay mugs of wine —enough to plow her under the table if she tried to finish it—and a steaming bowl of stew.

"The wine is quite acceptable, but I would exercise a degree of caution regarding the stew," Horatio winced as if it was bad memory.

She sipped at the wine and decided that if *this* was good wine, she'd definitely be avoiding the stew.

Betsy pinched herself, no change.

"Any chance that you'd know how badly I was injured or when I'm getting off these drugs? Or are you just a gorgeous hallucination named Horatio?"

Horatio hid a smile with a big draught of wine, but his blue eyes twinkled. They *actually* twinkled. It made him look very merry. If he really was in full elf-character, which his pointy ears indicated was likely, maybe it was part of his job to be merry. But that didn't explain how he'd made those pretty blue eyes twinkle. Of course "Elf: identification and interaction with" wasn't in any part of Delta Force's Operator Training Course.

Maybe she didn't want off these drugs, whatever they were. She'd had morphine after being shot up in Nigeria once and been completely loopy but calm as well. She still remembered portions of that helo ride while the combat search-and-rescue medics struggled to stabilize her. An incredibly handsome stranger, even in a seedy medieval pub, was a far more interesting reaction.

"I can place you back in Range 37 at any moment you should choose to request it. But I would like to discuss a special mission with you prior to such an eventuality."

"A special mission?" She tried the wine again while considering where he might have learned such speech patterns. British sit-coms came to mind. The second sip of wine slammed the back of her throat with its tannic bite. This time it only made her want to gag rather than rip her throat out, which was an improvement. She could also taste the high alcohol content. That, she decided, could be a good thing in the current situation and managed to brace herself through a third taste, but couldn't manage a fourth.

"Yes," Horatio spooned up some of the stew, apparently ignoring his earlier warning—at least until he put it in his mouth. Then looked as if he didn't know where to spit it out.

"In the fire."

He did so, creating a brief flurry of sparks.

"Back to my question," Betsy nudged her own stew bowl a little farther away as a safety precaution. "What *are* you and why am I hallucinating you?"

Not finding anywhere to wipe his mouth, he used his fingers, then wiped them on the edge of the table. "You are *not* hallucinating."

"Just what I'd expect a hallucination to say."

Horatio sighed before forging on. "This is real. Or mostly real. We see each other, but the locals merely observe a pair of strangers in locals' clothing."

"Uh-huh." Betsy could only assume this was one of those accidents that was bad enough for amnesia to kick in. Most of this she wouldn't mind losing, though Horatio himself was a real pleasure to look at. She'd been in the field a long time and dallying with a squad mate just wasn't an option. Horatio however... He looked far yummier than the wine.

What *had* happened?

Maybe a stone wall of Range 37 collapsed onto her? Or perhaps one of her shots at the metal targets had ricocheted back. At this point it wouldn't surprise if one of the targets had *shot* her back. Talking to a reindeer herding elf in a twelfth-century pub made anything seem possible.

"And as pertains to your earlier question, I am an elf

—of the Christmas variety. The one entrusted with the care of Santa's reindeer, if I may be specific."

"Hence, Horatio the Herder," Betsy didn't think her imagination was strange enough to cook up this one, which was tipping the scale—impossibly—toward the side of this experience being somehow real.

"Precisely. My dilemma lies in the fact that it is only three days to Christmas and I can not find the lead reindeer anywhere. I have need of aid from a professional."

"Me?"

"You."

"You need me to track down...Rudolph?"

"Well, his name is Jeremy, but essentially yes."

"Jeremy the red-nosed reindeer. Doesn't exactly have the right ring to it, does it?"

"Robert L. May was prone to agreeing with you, which is why he changed the name for the Montgomery Ward children's book he wrote regarding Jeremy's tribulations as a young reindeer."

"Wow!" Betsy managed a large swallow of wine to fortify herself. "You actually delivered all that as a straight line. I'm impressed." Then she stared down at the wine and wondered what exactly was in it that she almost believed him.

3

____

"So, lay it out for me."

"Lay *it* out? What needs laying out of it?"

Betsy pulled out her Benchmade Infidel knife, thumbed the release, and the four-inch, double-edged blade snapped out the front of the handle. She began carving the Special Operations Command shoulder patch into the wooden table with the point—a stylized arrowhead with a knife up the middle.

Horatio eyed her carefully. "I expect that you are a hard woman to buy Christmas presents for. What's your Christmas wish?"

"I gave up on wishes a long time ago."

Horatio looked at her aghast.

She held up the blade. The black-coated D2 steel appeared bloody in the dim firelight. "This one did nicely as a gift to myself. Start talking, Elf." She returned to her carving.

"We permit the reindeer to run wild during the summer season."

"I could do with a little running wild myself." Betsy could feel her inhibitions slipping away. She hadn't had that much wine. But knowing that you were injured and in some drug-induced dream made it difficult to care much about propriety. And if she was going to run a little wild, who better to do it with than a gorgeous man-elf-herder-thing.

"They always return when the fall lengthens the wavelengths that leaves reflect."

"Lengthens the wavelengths? Oh, reds and golds. Never mind. Keep going." Keeping her gaze averted from his intense eyes didn't help much. His slightly hoity-toity way of speaking didn't diminish the fact that his voice was just as beautiful as he was. She couldn't be so shallow that a beautiful man with a liquid voice was getting to her, even if he was.

"Jeremy has failed to return."

"That was the fall. And you're just contacting me three days before Christmas? That is not what we'd typically call adroit mission planning." She began digging the arch of the upper tab of the shoulder patch. What if she carved in the word "Airborne" as it should be and the table was discovered eight hundred years from now? Cause a hell of a stir. Perhaps she should drop into wherever this village was in the real world and find out for herself.

"Actually, yesterday was the final day of fall. We have now traversed the threshold of the winter solstice and such matters are suddenly come to a head."

"Maybe a hunter got him."

Horatio actually flinched. His oddly light complexion paled even further.

"Sorry, but you have to consider all of the possibilities."

"That is one I shall not be considering until all other hope is lost."

"So, where do we begin?" It wasn't often that an impossibly beautiful man asked her to do something so highly unlikely. Usually it was requests for sexual favors, which wasn't something she doled out to any Tom, Dick, or Horatio.

"At the stables, I suppose."

"Of course. Because why wouldn't Santa's reindeer have stables. Are you nuts, Horatio? I was thinking it was me, but maybe it's you."

"I have not considered the possibility," Horatio's beautiful brow actually furrowed for a long moment as he studied his wine, then shook his head, causing his hair to flutter attractively. "No, I find your premise unlikely."

Could she ever be with a man prettier than she was? If he looked like Horatio, in a heartbeat.

"Do elves kiss?" It was amazing what could be done within a drug-induced haze.

"We do," the color returned to his cheeks, brightly.

"Do they marry?"

"Is that a proposal, Betsy?"

Now it was her turn to scoff. "I just don't like my fantasies to already be married before I kiss them."

"Then you may do so without further concern if that is your wish." The bright color high on his cheeks wasn't going away, which was rather cute.

It would be a little like kissing a movie star. He was too perfect. But that wasn't exactly a complaint worth filing with the Fantasy Dream Department—a division of the US Army Personnel Services Branch she'd never thought of submitting a requisition request to before.

Betsy reached across the table to snag the lapel of his body-hugging black leather suit and pulled him closer. She leaned in and briefly tasted the mutton stew on his lips. Thankfully, she was past that before it could put her off completely. Past that, he tasted of cinnamon and the wild outdoors of a snowy night. Of luscious hot cocoa and a crackling fire.

Horatio's kiss was warm, attentive, thoughtful...and masterful.

If she hadn't been dreaming before, she most certainly was now. Dreaming of how fast they could go somewhere there weren't any other people, just the two of them and a big, warm bed.

Her pulse was soon chattering faster than an M134 Minigun on full auto, yet Horatio was still only exploring the first steps of a kiss.

"Get me out of here," her own voice sounded desperate and needy.

"As you wish."

4

———

THE COLD SLAPPED HER SO HARD THAT SHE LOST HER breath—as well as her lip lock on Horatio.

"What the hell?"

"The stables."

"You brought me to a freezing cold barn?"

"I brought you to the source as you requested. These are the reindeer stables of St. Nicholas of Myra."

Betsy could only look around in astonishment. A long line of stalls appeared to be made out of living yew trees, all trained into walls and stable dividers. Their roots were lost beneath a luxuriant layer of living grass—the brightest green she'd ever seen. The stables were lit by fireflies swarming among the branches.

And the sky.

The ceiling was of glass so clear that she could hardly tell it was there between her and the magnificent night sky. As she blinked away the worst of the pub's smoke and her eyes adjusted, she began picking out constellations.

"That's the North Star."

Horatio looked up as well. "It is."

"It's directly overhead."

"Point six seven degrees from directly overhead to be precise. We are at the celestial north pole rather than the magnetic or geographic one. Nice, isn't it?"

"But the North Pole isn't over land. It's over sea ice."

"It is, in most planes of reality."

Betsy couldn't think of what else to do...so she hit him. Not hard—it had been a very nice kiss after all. Just squarely enough in the solar plexus that he wouldn't be able to speak for a few moments so that she could do some thinking.

Horatio dropped to his knees and wheezed a bit.

North Pole.

A missing reindeer named Jeremy.

An elf, a very handsome elf who could kiss better than any human—a kiss that also left her wondering what else he could do better.

St. Nicholas beneath Polaris the North Star in some very adjacent reality.

Real? Surreal? Digital? Drugs?

No way to tell.

She sighed, and helped Horatio back to his feet.

The only way out is through. Old axiom. There were times she hated old axioms.

"Last spring. Did anyone see which way Jeremy went?"

5

———

IT HAD TAKEN THE CIA YEARS TO FIND BIN LADEN. AND another half-year to actually get around to taking him down after "Maya" had found him.

She had three days to track a reindeer. Her total assets? One elf who didn't want it to be known that he'd lost Santa's most famous reindeer, Jeremy.

The first break came when they were questioning the other reindeer. They didn't like having her around and were very standoffish, until she dug around in Horatio's larder and found a bag of carrots. They warmed up to her quickly after that. Who knew that reindeer had a major weak spot for carrots.

A small portion of St. Nick's deer herd—mostly the younger set—had gone south and west last spring, rather than south and east to their normal habitat in Finland. It turned out that reindeer had a particularly low-brow sense of humor—even worse than most Delta operators. They liked spending their summers mingling with the Finnish herds and teasing them about not making the cut to become a Christmas reindeer. They also weren't above tripping them into mudholes and the like.

The breakaway herd had crossed down over the Canadian tundra, mingling with the caribou herds in some sort of convention. But they quickly grew bored as the Canadians had even less of a sense of humor than their Finnish counterparts.

That had led to any number of fights and endless head butting. The younger members of the herd whined about it no end.

"Teenagers," she scoffed to Horatio after he'd translated that for her. "Hard to deal with."

"Gift cards." Apparently that was his harshest epithet. "It is the only way St. Nick has found to deal with them at Christmas."

Betsy had been such a good girl as a teen, of course taking care of her ailing mother had made that an obvious choice. She'd even been well behaved as an Army grunt then a Delta operator. And now, just three days from freedom, she'd been injured and was drugged up in some Fort Bragg hospital. It didn't seem fair.

She tossed out some more carrots to get the rest of the story. Most had continued west to roam with the big herds in Alaska. But Jeremy had turned south once more, toward the heat and bright sun. He'd said he was headed to a place called Mont-a-land or something like. None of them had ever heard of it.

"Montana?"

Some of them thought that sounded right, but were more interested in carrots than answering questions. She took the bag with her when she left. When they protested, she simply made a show of resettling her rifle across her shoulders...which proved most effective. About time they did some growing up.

She and Horatio started in the Canadian Northwest Territories at a place with the unlikely name of Reindeer Station. Eight or nine houses located along the edge of the sprawling Mackenzie River delta less than fifty miles from the Arctic Ocean. It wasn't all that much warmer than the North Pole with just two days to Christmas. The river was iced over and was crisscrossed with snowmobile tracks. She'd borrowed a brilliant red parka with a white sheepskin lining to keep her warm.

It took most of the morning to track the region's sole remaining reindeer herder to his remote cabin. It was a gruesome affair. Not merely well away from even the hamlet of Reindeer Station, it was also the butchery for bulls thinned from the herd. Reindeer meat was stacked outside in the Arctic chill and quick-frozen beneath hides. Inside the hut, the tools of the trade dangled from hooks on the wall. Yet the herder also had a young reindeer on a leash as a pet.

Horatio was shivering even more than the temperature could account for.

Betsy held his hand tightly to calm him, which she didn't mind doing at all, while she was talking to the man. Even while shivering from disgust or distress, Horatio's hand was as warm as a handmade quilt. He appeared perfectly comfortable in his body-hugging leather despite the Arctic temperature.

The herder's English was limited and apparently Horatio was only fluent in English, French, and reindeer, so he was of no help. The herder, speaking mostly in some Inuit language, allowed as he might have seen a rather curious animal that had stood aloof from his herd of three thousand reindeer. A magnificent bull with more points than he could count. He waved south.

"Inuvik?" That was the next town, some twenty miles away.

He shook his head and waved again.

"Fort McPherson?" It was the only other town she knew in the Northwest Territories.

Again the wave south, "Mont-a-land."

6

BUT GOING DIRECTLY TO MONTANA WAS TOO BIG A LEAP. IT would take forever to pick up Jeremy's track again. So they worked south in stages following the rumors of an aloof, many-pointed bull reindeer.

"I thought Jeremy was supposed to be a cute little guy."

"Indeed he was, seventy-five years ago when Robert L. May wrote about him. He has matured somewhat over the years. He is still a sweetheart though as he never allowed the success to go to his head."

"How long do reindeer usually live? Maybe he died of old age."

"Fifteen to twenty years, typically, unless they are in the employ of St. Nicholas. Then their lives are rather extended."

Betsy eyed him carefully. There was an agelessness to Horatio's clear features. He would have been as classically handsome a thousand years ago as he was now. Perhaps there were some questions that it was better not to ask.

Besides, time was running too fast.

"Can't you slow it down?"

"Not even St. Nicholas can do that."

Thirty-six hours remaining.

Jeremy wanted her to eat something after they'd chased leads all the way down the frozen Mackenzie to the small town of Yellowknife on Great Slave Lake. From there, they'd run the ice road over to the hamlet of Detah and were now sitting in a small barn. The owner had told the story of the most "magnificent bull" he'd ever tracked while hunting. Best he'd ever seen, but apparently his shot had gone wild.

"Jeremy is very wily," Horatio's whisper had tickled her ear like a warm breeze.

She tried a carrot, but they'd frozen hard. "Give me an MRE and let's get going."

So, he gave her a pre-heated Meal-Ready-to-Eat. She didn't ask how. Next time she'd ask for a roast beef dinner with Yorkshire pudding and see if her friendly neighborhood hallucination could deliver.

"Maybe you should rest." The small barn had a hayloft, and the hunter had returned to his ice fishing on the frozen lake. It was tempting. So very, very tempting. She couldn't remember the last time she'd been this tired.

"When the mission is done." She chowed down on the Southwest Beef and Black Beans while Horatio massaged her shoulders. Now that was something she could become very used to—far better than the cold, lack of sleep, and the utterly ludicrous situation.

His fingers were strong enough to ease even her soldier-hard muscles until she felt ready to melt against him. She tossed aside the empty MRE package and decided that a little melting wasn't completely outside the mission profile.

She'd forgotten—mostly—about the kiss in the ancient French bistro. The memory did nothing to prepare her for what happened next. Horatio felt luscious as he pulled her tightly against him. In mid-clench, she tried to rub herself even more tightly against his incredible body.

Horatio grunted, and not in a good way.

"Your vest," he managed to gasp.

Betsy paused and looked down between them. She wore her Glock sidearm, as most Delta did, front and center for a fast draw. Above that, pockets of ammo and emergency supplies made hard edges that had left scrapes on his smooth leather.

"Sorry." Vest. Mission. Ludicrous scenario.

The only way out is through.

She sighed, sat up, and patted Horatio's cheek. He had the decency to look disappointed despite the gouges she'd been digging into his chest.

"Your colonel," Horatio nodded to the south, "said that you were the hardest-driving scout in his entire team."

"You spoke to Colonel Gibson about finding one of Santa's reindeer?" She tried to imagine how the stern colonel took it.

"Perhaps I may not have asked him quite directly, but he was very impressed with your skills."

That was news to her. She hadn't known that Delta Force's commander even knew who she was.

She sighed to herself that some overwound inner drive wouldn't even let her enjoy a hallucinatory snuggle.

They left the tiny Detah barn and they turned south across Alberta.

7

———

THEY HAD PIZZA IN BANFF AND SHE SPENT THREE DELICIOUS hours mostly passed out in the curve of Horatio's arms in a snowed-in hiking cabin high in Glacier Park. She didn't ask how Horatio moved them from place to place. It seemed that they flowed, glided, perhaps simply morphed from one destination to the next. It was a dream, so it was easy to not question the transitions.

But she would miss her time with Horatio. No, she'd miss Horatio himself. Even strung out on whatever narcotic was giving her this extended dream, she was becoming very attached to him.

Yes, he'd started out all strange and mysterious and mostly concerned about a missing reindeer. But he had shifted. More slowly than their jumping from one place to another, but just as steadily.

Still wrapped in her parka, she lay in his arms in the chill cabin and felt...right. As if it was where she was supposed to be. Perhaps "content" was a better word, though it was not one that had ever come up before in her life.

He hadn't asked about her past, which was just as well. She didn't want to talk about it. But neither had he talked about his. Did elves have pasts? Did elves have regrets? She hoped not as she had enough for both of them.

"What is an elf's life like?" She could feel him shift as if he was looking down at the top of her head in some surprise.

"Normal enough. The reindeer usually do a good job of taking care of themselves, that's why I didn't think to worry. Generally I spend but one month a year tending them. It's a good life for them as well." And he began telling her about their grazing habits, and the practical jokes they liked to play.

One year they'd started at the South Pole rather than the North, forcing St. Nicholas to act like a Dumpster-diver as he dug out successive presents from the bottom of the sleigh's pile instead of working top-down. Or the year they'd switched all of the rabbits' stockings with all of the squirrels'—the rabbits had ended up having a grand game of ice hockey with the acorns and walnuts but the squirrels had never figured out what to do with the sudden bounty of cabbage.

It was only as they were trekking south into the Flathead Wilderness of Montana that she realized he'd told her nothing of himself. Perhaps it was fair, she'd said nothing of herself either, but it rankled. Of course, with his voice, she'd happily listen to him reading the naughty and nice name list—especially the naughty if he gave some of the details.

Dawn broke hard.

She couldn't think of how else to describe it. While traveling through Canada, they had been in and out of snowstorms beneath gray skies. This morning, they'd left the cabin in Glacier Park beneath the last stars of the night, almost as brightly perfect as those from Santa's reindeer stables. It had been a relief that the North Star had shifted well down the sky, so they were indeed well to the south.

But standing atop the Castle Reef ridgeline and looking down at the Montana Front Range in one direction, and up into the heart of the snow-capped Rocky Mountains in the other, dawn began with a snap as sharp as the cold.

The sun lanced over the flat horizon from impossibly far away and the entire world was catapulted into a limitless blue bowl of sky.

"I take it this is why they call it Big Sky country," Horatio sounded breathless.

"I guess." Betsy also couldn't catch her breath. It might be the eight-thousand-foot elevation or the slicing cold of the morning wind driving ice crystals into her face like blowback from Barrett .50 cal sniper rifle.

It might be the view.

But it was more the realization that this was December 23rd. One way or another, their quest would be over today. As soon as sunset hit the International Date Line in roughly twelve hours, St. Nicholas would be flying off to do his job—with or without the errant Jeremy.

Yet she could feel that he was close. Some instinct, honed over the years by Delta training, told her their quarry was nearly in sight.

She flagged down a rancher passing by in his helicopter, who settled it neatly atop the peak. Clearly ex-military by how he flew, despite the fact that he now commanded a small Bell JetRanger with a herd of horses painted along the side.

"How can I help you, ma'am?" He drawled it out in a Texas accent so fake that it would get him lynched in certain states. "Need a lift off this here hilltop?"

"No, we're fine."

"We?" He tugged his mirrored sunglasses down enough to squint at her strangely.

She glanced aside at Horatio who just shook his head.

Fine. Whatever. So he was invisible or something. Had he shown up for anyone else, or had she just crossed Canada as a solo crazy lady talking to herself? She'd bet on the latter, but didn't have time to deal with it now.

"Have you seen a reindeer that—"

"Reindeer? We have moose and elk in these parts. Even a few caribou, but no reindeer."

"Reindeer and caribou are the same animal," Horatio prompted her.

When the pilot didn't respond, she repeated the information.

"Wa'll, ain't that a wonder."

"Have you seen a particularly impressive one lately?"

He rubbed his chin thoughtfully. He'd have been the

handsomest man in any crowd that didn't include Horatio.

"Might have heard mention of one. Over to a hot spring up along the North Fork Deep Creek. My wife said she saw one when one of our guides and a guest shot—"

"Shot?" Betsy grabbed the pilot's arm in a panic.

"Shot two *young* bulls," the man looked down at his arm in some distress and tried to shake her off. At least the awful Texas accent was gone.

She shook him by his arm to keep him talking.

"She said it was the biggest old bull she'd ever seen. Had himself a couple of does and a fawn. Guess they didn't want to break up the family. Ease off, lady." He wiggled his arm a little and grimaced.

"Jeremy has a family?" Horatio's blue eyes were almost as wide as the Big Sky. Then he looked at her and his gaze shifted as if asking if she also had a family.

She had no one. No one on the outside, and in just another day, she'd be out of Delta and have no one on the inside either. This definitely was *not* the moment she wanted to be thinking about her future.

"Do you know where that hot spring is?"

Horatio nodded.

"Of course I do," the pilot looked at her strangely. "I'm the one who just told you about it. Are you okay all alone up here?"

"Not really." She let go of the pilot who began massaging the arm she'd had a hold of. She was hunting for one of Santa's reindeer and absolutely falling for a hallucination named Horatio, but she didn't want to talk about it with some rancher pilot. "But I can find it on my own."

"I can't just leave you here, lady." The pilot looked around. There was nothing to see from the summit of Castle Reef except snowy mountains, dusky plains, and the biggest blue sky ever.

"Fine, *I'll* leave *you,* then. Thanks for the help."

She walked past Horatio. For the first time, she could feel one of his spatial shifts slowly wrapping around her before it actually happened.

"What the hell?"

She liked that she left the pilot with his own hallucination to figure out. Misery loves company.

8

————

THE HOT SPRING WAS UNOCCUPIED, BUT IT DIDN'T TAKE HER long to pick up the fresh tracks through the snow.

"By the tracks, it's a big bull, two does, and a half-grown fawn."

Horatio let her lead the way. It was a hard slog through the deep snow, even though the herd had broken the path.

At one point, an avalanche had erased their tracks. It took them several anxious hours to pick them up again on the far side of the damage path.

It was barely an hour to local sunset—and only four or five to Global Flying Time—when she found them. The small herd was grazing near a copse of Douglas fir that had blocked much of the snow. They were kicking aside the little snow that remained and eating the frozen grass.

"Jeremy!" Horatio's shout of joy shook loose an entire cascade of snow from one of the trees that she barely managed to dodge.

The two of them—elf and reindeer—ran to each other and were soon chattering away in reindeer which sounded like grunts and squeaks to her untrained ear.

Betsy ducked under the low-hanging branches and found a small spot clear of snow where she could lean back against the trunk and wait.

Exhaustion rippled through her as it always did after a hard scouting job. But it wasn't just that. She was leaving Delta because she could feel that she was losing the edge and, with how far past it Delta normally operated, that was an unacceptable change. One far too prone to death. For the first time since she'd joined the Army, she didn't belong anywhere. Yet over the last three days...

Betsy watched Horatio as he was introduced to the rest of Jeremy's family.

For the last three days, Betsy had started to belong. Not merely due to her skills either. When she was with Horatio even something as crazy as searching for Santa's missing reindeer made sense. Anything...*everything* somehow made sense when she was with him. She hadn't truly belonged somewhere that she could ever recall, but she could see herself belonging with a fantasy named Horatio.

She must have dozed, though the sun had barely shifted when Horatio kissed her awake. That gained her undivided attention, but he was too excited for it to last more than a moment.

"He has a family. But he couldn't get them back to the stables on his own. He needed an elfin herder to transport them the first time. Jeremy is a good man—"

"Reindeer," she corrected him.

"Reindeer," Horatio readily agreed and kissed her on the nose. "He didn't want to abandon his family, but didn't know any of the locals who could send me a message. Apparently love at first sight happens for reindeer as well."

As well? Is that what had happened to her? It didn't seem very likely, but neither did anything in the three days since she'd last stood on Range 37.

Now Horatio was looking at her very intently. "You're the most amazing human I've ever met, Betsy."

"Human?" But that said nothing of the amazing elf women he'd surely known. Why was she pining for a drug-dream fantasy?

"Woman. Of any breed or species. I've been watching you for days and can't believe your tenacity and skill. Or your beauty. Can all human women kiss the way you do?"

Betsy could feel herself becoming overwhelmed by his compliments. But nothing overwhelmed a Delta soldier. They were trained to keep their thoughts under control in any situation.

She slipped her fingers into his magnificent mane of hair and tugged it lightly to pull him closer.

"Perhaps I won't give you any excuse to find out."

"Mmm," he made a happy sound as he leaned into her kiss.

She could feel it supercharge her, ramp her up even the way a decisive victory couldn't achieve. There was a feeling of vitality, of joyous triumph at being alive at the end of a hard battle.

Horatio made her feel that ten times over. His kiss

filled her thoughts until they overflowed and radiated back to him. She wanted him to take her right here, right now. Under the trees. In the snow. Even with the reindeer watching. She didn't care.

She opened her eyes to look up into his amazing eyes the color of the Montana Big Sky, just as a particularly large snowflake plastered itself across her shooting goggles she didn't recall putting back on.

It left a wet smear when she brushed it aside.

And once again she was in the heart of a mock Afghan village, dusted with North Carolina snow.

A mannequin bearing an RPG leaned out of a doorway.

Only habit had her shooting it twice in the face and once in the chest.

9

Betsy finished the Range 37 course with the same high marks she always did, but felt none of the victory at the score—even though she'd managed to snatch-and-grab the bad guy on her own.

The next two days were a slow slog through the bureaucracy of leaving a service she'd given a decade to. Quartermaster this. Housing that. Personnel records the other thing.

She couldn't equate the Range 37 exercise and the two days of bureaucracy involved in leaving the service with the three days she'd spent with Horatio the Herder tracking a stray Christmas reindeer.

At each step she took through her Fort Bragg reality over the same three days, she could feel the other reality fading into memory. The three days with Horatio had passed so quickly and now time crawled.

December 21st: Quartermaster this. Horatio's strong hands resting on her shoulders a moment longer than needed as he helped her into a red-and-white parka while they stood in the most magnificent stables she'd ever seen.

December 22nd: Housing that. Holding each other close in a small hayloft in Detah on the frozen shores of the Great Slave Lake. A feeling of belonging she'd never known.

December 23rd: Personnel records the other thing. Waking in his arms in a Glacier Park cabin and knowing she had never been anywhere so safe or so...important before in her life.

December 24th: nothing but a blur. Horatio the elf would be with his reindeer, making sure they performed their annual flight, preparing the stable for their return. Bedding them down when they were done.

No one that she'd served with was currently rotated into Fort Bragg from abroad, so she passed her final days in the US military in silence. Alone.

The snow had melted and new teams were working their way through Range 37. No twelfth-century French village with bad wine and poisonous stew would be awaiting them any more than it was awaiting her. She'd go back if she could, just to see Horatio once more. Once she was out, maybe she'd take her motorcycle to Europe and go searching for a French pub with an Airborne shoulder patch carved into one table's surface.

But there wouldn't be. Hallucinations didn't work that way. It had taken a long and lonely Christmas eve to convince herself that was all it had been.

Early Christmas morning, she turned in her firearm, was issued her DD 214 Honorable Discharge form, and was issued a temporary visitor badge that would see her to the front gates. She bundled up against the chilly day, missing the warmth of the North Pole parka, though she didn't really feel the cold anymore. Climbing on her Yamaha YZF superbike, Betsy rolled out the Manchester Gate by Pope Airfield.

Maybe she'd swing south and see a bit of the country. She had no real plans until summer. But then her course would be certain. This summer, she'd be chasing the melting snow north, starting with the Flathead Wilderness. Even if it hadn't been real, she'd retrace the path as far north as she possibly could, right up to Reindeer Station on the banks of the Mackenzie River.

Perhaps there would be a reindeer, a small fawn grown into the grand bull that would at least remind her of Jeremy and she could pretend that he would lead her north to a stable made of yew trees.

At the Fort Bragg gate, the corporal took her temporary pass, and saluted her smartly. She returned the gesture for the last time, then rolled out the gate. Out Manchester Road, she'd pick up North Bragg Boulevard and punch south.

For now.

Then she'd—

Betsy slammed on the brakes and tried to make sense of what she was seeing.

Just off base, along the wooded lane, stood Pyrates Sports Bar. It wasn't much of a place: pool, beer, and a decent burger.

And leaning against one of the big maples stood an impossibly thin man with black hair down to his waist and eyes the color of the Big Sky.

She couldn't release her death grip on the handlebars as Horatio strolled up to her and reached out to raise the visor on her helmet.

"Hi."

"Hi? *Hi!* That's what you have to say for yourself? I've spent three days convincing myself that you were just a hallucination. What are you doing to me? Is this some kind of weird drug experiment or—"

Horatio leaned in and kissed her.

She dropped the clutch. The Yamaha lurched then stalled, and broke the kiss. She'd already forgotten his taste of cinnamon and the great outdoors. How had she possibly forgotten that?

"Does that feel like a hallucination in your consideration?"

Betsy could only shake her head.

"I know this is a little abrupt, but how would you like a job?"

"No way, Horatio. You evaporated at the end of the last one."

"I would not this time."

"And I'm supposed to trust an elf hallucination on that?"

"Absolutely," and Horatio's smile lit his eyes to a merry twinkle, just as they did every time.

"Why?"

"Because I could use the assistance of a skilled reindeer herder."

"You want me to live at the North Pole with you?"

"We would travel a lot. I only tend the reindeer

around Christmas. An elf's main job during the year is rather global: spreading good cheer wherever he can."

"Can you promise me that you're not a hallucination? I really want you to not be a hallucination." Even if he was, Betsy had the feeling that she wasn't going to care.

"I've been wracking my brain to find an appropriate Christmas present for you. That wish will do nicely. I promise you that I am completely real."

She hadn't thought about a Christmas wish in a long time, but if there was ever one she wanted to come true...

Betsy kissed him lightly, then nodded toward the back of the bike.

"Climb aboard, Horatio. We've got some good cheer to spread."

10

———

Betsy leaned against the yew tree that made one side of the stable's main door and pulled her red-and-white parka more tightly about her as she watched Horatio with the herd. It was Christmas Eve and once more the excitement practically shimmered through St. Nick's stables.

Harnesses with bright polished bells were laid upon well-curry-combed backs as the reindeer pranced with delight. A small elf choir stood up in the hayloft singing about Good King Wenceslas, Little Drummer Boys, and Friendly Beasts. She noted that Rudolph was nowhere in the repertoire—Jeremy was *not* a fan of Robert L. May. He'd grown to be a very dignified reindeer.

"Especially now that he has a family to look after," Horatio had whispered softly in her ear one night.

And his nose was definitely not red, his main point of contention.

Before Jeremy was harnessed into the lead position, he clopped over to her and faced her silently.

Betsy's grasp of reindeer language still sucked, though she was improving.

But he didn't say a word.

Instead, he tipped his head down, and shifted his face gently against her chest and simply rested it there. His great rack of antlers framed her protectively to either side.

She hugged him, wrapping her arms around his head.

"Merry Christmas to all," she whispered to him. "And have a good flight."

He snorted a soft laugh at her twisting of the last line of Rudolph's story before pulling away to stride over to his position to be harnessed in.

With a stamp and snort and a prance and a paw, the herd was soon aloft, towing St. Nick and his sleigh on their merry rounds.

The silence seemed to be a long time settling over the stables once they were gone. But in time, even the fireflies had settled and only the quiet stars of the Arctic night lit the stables.

Horatio slipped close beside her and wrapped his arms about her. She rested back against him and marveled at how her life had changed. How she would never be alone again.

Last Christmas, Horatio had given her a gift beyond imagining, she was no longer alone in the world.

She rested her hand on her own belly.

Tomorrow, Christmas morning—after the reindeer had completed their flight, then gone to bed for the night —she would tell him the news.

Her gift to him would be—she tried not to think it in the same rhythm as the Rudolph poem, but being married to a Christmas elf was changing her in many wondrous ways—that quite soon they'd be three.

LAST WORDS

I wrote four novels and eleven stories exploring Delta Force.

Yes, they're romances and perhaps over-idealized, but I feel as if I personally better understand these silent warriors who defend my country in ways I can't imagine (and will mostly never hear about).

When I set out to tell these stories, I wanted to explore their life choices, and honor them and what they do.

Thank you so much for joining me on that exploration.

I can only hope that you've enjoyed it even half as much as I have.

Aim high!
M. L. Buchman
North Shore, MA 2020

OFF THE LEASH (EXCERPT)

"You're joking."

"Nope. That's his name. And he's yours now."

Sergeant Linda Hamlin wondered quite what it would take to wipe that smile off Lieutenant Jurgen's face. A 120mm round from an M1A1 Abrams Main Battle Tank came to mind.

The kennel master of the US Secret Service's Canine Team was clearly a misogynistic jerk from the top of his polished head to the bottoms of his equally polished boots. She wondered if the shoelaces were polished as well.

Then she looked over at the poor dog sitting hopefully on the concrete kennel floor. His stall had a dog bed three times his size and a water bowl deep enough for him to bathe in. No toys, because toys always came from the handler as a reward. He offered her a sad sigh and a liquid doggy gaze. The kennel even smelled wrong, more of sanitizer than dog. The walls seemed to echo with each bark down the long line of kennels housing the candidate hopefuls for the next addition to the Secret Service's team.

Thor—really?—was a brindle-colored mutt, part who-knew and part no-one-cared. He looked like a cross between an oversized, long-haired schnauzer and a dust mop that someone had spilled dark gray paint on. After mixing in streaks of tawny brown, they'd left one white paw just to make him all the more laughable.

And of course Lieutenant Jerk Jurgen would assign Thor to the first woman on the USSS K-9 team.

Unable to resist, she leaned over far enough to scruff the dog's ears. He was the physical opposite of the sleek and powerful Malinois MWDs—military war dogs—that she'd been handling for the 75th Rangers for the last five years. They twitched with eagerness and nerves. A good MWD was seventy pounds of pure drive—every damn second of the day. If the mild-mannered Thor weighed thirty pounds, she'd be surprised. And he looked like a little girl's best friend who should have a pink bow on his collar.

Jurgen was clearly ex-Marine and would have no respect for the Army. Of course, having been in the Army's Special Operations Forces, she knew better than to respect a Marine.

"We won't let any old swabbie bother us, will we?"

Jurgen snarled—definitely Marine Corps. Swabbie was slang for a Navy sailor and a Marine always took offense at being lumped in with them no matter how much they belonged. Of course the swabbies took offense at having the Marines lumped with *them*. Too bad there weren't any Navy around so that she could get two for the price of one. Jurgen wouldn't be her boss, so appeasing him wasn't high on her to-do list.

At least she wouldn't need any of the protective bite gear working with Thor. With his stature, he was an explosives detection dog without also being an attack one.

"Where was he trained?" She stood back up to face the beast.

"Private outfit in Montana—some place called Henderson's Ranch. Didn't make their MWD program," his scoff said exactly what he thought the likelihood of any dog outfit in Montana being worthwhile. "They wanted us to try the little runt out."

She'd never heard of a training program in Montana. MWDs all came out of Lackland Air Force Base training. The Secret Service mostly trained their own and they all came from Vohne Liche Kennels in Indiana. Unless... Special Operations Forces dogs were trained by private contractors. She'd worked beside a Delta Force dog for a single month—he'd been incredible.

"Is he trained in English or German?" Most American MWDs were trained in German so that there was no confusion in case a command word happened to be part of a spoken sentence. It also made it harder for any random person on the battlefield to shout something that would confuse the dog.

"German according to his paperwork, but he won't listen to me much in either language."

Might as well give the diminutive Thor a few basic tests. A snap of her fingers and a slap on her thigh had the dog dropping into a smart "heel" position. No need to call out *Fuss—by my foot.*

"*Pass auf!*" *Guard!* She made a pistol with her thumb and forefinger and aimed it at Jurgen as she grabbed her forearm with her other hand—the military hand sign for enemy.

The little dog snarled at Jurgen sharply enough to have him backing out of the kennel. "Goddamn it!"

"*Ruhig.*" *Quiet.* Thor maintained his fierce posture but dropped the snarl.

"*Gute Hund.*" *Good dog,* Linda countered the command.

Thor looked up at her and wagged his tail happily. She tossed him a doggie treat, which he caught midair and crunched happily.

She didn't bother looking up at Jurgen as she knelt once more to check over the little dog. His scruffy fur was so soft that it tickled. Good strength in the jaw, enough to show he'd had bite training despite his size—perfect if she ever needed to take down a three-foot-tall terrorist. Legs said he was a jumper.

"Take your time, Hamlin. I've got nothing else to do with the rest of my goddamn day except babysit you and this mutt."

"Is the course set?"

"Sure. Take him out," Jurgen's snarl sounded almost as nasty as Thor's before he stalked off.

She stood and slapped a hand on her opposite shoulder.

Thor sprang aloft as if he was attached to springs and she caught him easily. He'd cleared well over double his own height. Definitely trained...and far easier to catch than seventy pounds of hyperactive Malinois.

She plopped him back down on the ground. On lead or off? She'd give him the benefit of the doubt and try off first to see what happened.

Linda zipped up her brand-new USSS jacket against the cold and led the way out of the kennel into the hard sunlight of the January morning. Snow had brushed the higher hills around the USSS James J. Rowley Training Center—which this close to Washington, DC, wasn't saying much—but was melting quickly. Scents wouldn't carry as well on the cool air, making it more of a challenge for Thor to locate the explosives. She didn't know where they were either. The course was a test for handler as well as dog.

Jurgen would be up in the observer turret looking for any excuse to mark down his newest team. Perhaps teasing him about being just a Marine hadn't been her best tactical choice. She sighed. At least she was consistent—she'd always been good at finding ways to piss people off before she could stop herself and consider the wisdom of doing so.

This test was the culmination of a crazy three months, so she'd forgive herself this time—something she also wasn't very good at.

In October she'd been out of the Army and unsure what to do next. Tucked in the packet with her DD 214 honorable discharge form had been a flyer on career opportunities with the US Secret Service dog team: *Be all your dog can be!* No one else being released from Fort

Benning that day had received any kind of a job flyer at all that she'd seen, so she kept quiet about it.

She had to pass through DC on her way back to Vermont—her parent's place. Burlington would work for, honestly, not very long at all, but she lacked anywhere else to go after a decade of service. So, she'd stopped off in DC to see what was up with that job flyer. Five interviews and three months to complete a standard six-month training course later—which was mostly a cakewalk after fighting with the US Rangers—she was on-board and this chill January day was her first chance with a dog. First chance to prove that she still had it. First chance to prove that she hadn't made a mistake in deciding that she'd seen enough bloodshed and war zones for one lifetime and leaving the Army.

The Start Here sign made it obvious where to begin, but she didn't dare hesitate to take in her surroundings past a quick glimpse. Jurgen's score would count a great deal toward where she and Thor were assigned in the future. Mostly likely on some field prep team, clearing the way for presidential visits.

As usual, hindsight informed her that harassing the lieutenant hadn't been an optimal strategy. A hindsight that had served her equally poorly with regular Army commanders before she'd finally hooked up with the Rangers—kowtowing to officers had never been one of her strengths.

Thankfully, the Special Operations Forces hadn't given a damn about anything except performance and *that* she could always deliver, since the day she'd been named the team captain for both soccer and volleyball.

She was never popular, but both teams had made all-state her last two years in school.

The canine training course at James J. Rowley was a two-acre lot. A hard-packed path of tramped-down dirt led through the brown grass. It followed a predictable pattern from the gate to a junker car, over to tool shed, then a truck, and so on into a compressed version of an intersection in a small town. Beyond it ran an urban street of gray clapboard two- and three-story buildings and an eight-story office tower, all without windows. Clearly a playground for Secret Service training teams.

Her target was the town, so she blocked the city street out of her mind. Focus on the problem: two roads, twenty storefronts, six houses, vehicles, pedestrians.

It might look normal...normalish with its missing windows and no movement. It would be anything but. Stocked with fake IEDs, a bombmaker's stash, suicide cars, weapons caches, and dozens of other traps, all waiting for her and Thor to find. He had to be sensitive to hundreds of scents and it was her job to guide him so that he didn't miss the opportunity to find and evaluate each one.

There would be easy scents, from fertilizer and diesel fuel used so destructively in the 1995 Oklahoma City bombing, to almost as obvious TNT to the very difficult to detect C-4 plastic explosive.

Mannequins on the street carried grocery bags and briefcases. Some held fresh meat, a powerful smell demanding any dog's attention, but would count as a false lead if they went for it. On the job, an explosives detection dog wasn't supposed to care about anything except explosives. Other mannequins were wrapped in suicide vests loaded with Semtex or wearing knapsacks filled with package bombs made from Russian PVV-5A.

She spotted Jurgen stepping into a glassed-in observer turret atop the corner drugstore. Someone else was already there and watching.

She looked down once more at the ridiculous little dog and could only hope for the best.

"Thor?"

He looked up at her.

She pointed to the left, away from the beaten path.

"*Such!*" *Find.*

Thor sniffed left, then right. Then he headed forward quickly in the direction she pointed.

CLIVE ANDREWS SAT IN THE SECOND-STORY WINDOW AT THE corner of Main and First, the only two streets in town. Downstairs was a drugstore all rigged to explode, except there were no triggers and there was barely enough explosive to blow up a candy box.

Not that he'd know, but that's what Lieutenant Jurgen had promised him.

It didn't really matter if it was rigged to blow for real, because when Miss Watson—never Ms. or Mrs.—asked for a "favor," you did it. At least he did. Actually, he had yet to meet anyone else who knew her. Not that he'd asked around. She wasn't the sort of person one talked about with strangers, or even close friends. He'd bet even if they did, it would be in whispers. That's just what she was like.

So he'd traveled across town from the White House and into Maryland on a cold winter's morning, barely past a sunrise that did nothing to warm the day. Now he sat in an unheated glass icebox and watched a new officer run a test course he didn't begin to understand. Lieutenant Jurgen settled in beside him at a console with feeds from a dozen cameras and banks of switches.

While waiting, Clive had been fooling around with a sketch on a small pad of paper. The next State Dinner was in seven days. President Zachary Taylor had invited the leaders of Vietnam, Japan, and the Philippines to the White House for discussions about some Chinese islands. Or something like that, Clive hadn't really been paying attention to the details past the attendee list.

Instead, he was contemplating the dessert for such a dinner that would surprise, perhaps delight, as well as being an icebreaker for future discussions. Being the chocolatier for the White House was the most exciting job he'd ever had.

Keep reading at fine retailers everywhere:
Off the Leash

ABOUT THE AUTHOR

USA Today and Amazon #1 Bestseller M. L. "Matt" Buchman started writing on a flight south from Japan to ride his bicycle across the Australian Outback. Just part of a solo around-the-world trip that ultimately launched his writing career.

From the very beginning, his powerful female heroines insisted on putting character first, *then* a great adventure. He's since written over 60 action-adventure thrillers and military romantic suspense novels. And just for the fun of it: 100 short stories, and a fast-growing pile of read-by-author audiobooks.

Booklist says: "3X Top 10 of the Year." PW says: "Tom Clancy fans open to a strong female lead will clamor for more." His fans say: "I want more now...of everything." That his characters are even more insistent than his fans is a hoot.

As a 30-year project manager with a geophysics degree who has designed and built houses, flown and jumped out of planes, and solo-sailed a 50' ketch, he is awed by what is possible. More at: www.mlbuchman.com.

Other works by M. L. Buchman: *(* - also in audio)*

Thrillers

Dead Chef
One Chef!
Two Chef!

Miranda Chase
*Drone**
*Thunderbolt**
*Condor**
*Ghostrider**

Romantic Suspense

Delta Force
*Target Engaged**
*Heart Strike**
*Wild Justice**
*Midnight Trust**

Firehawks
MAIN FLIGHT
Pure Heat
Full Blaze
*Hot Point**
*Flash of Fire**
Wild Fire

SMOKEJUMPERS
*Wildfire at Dawn**
*Wildfire at Larch Creek**
*Wildfire on the Skagit**

The Night Stalkers
MAIN FLIGHT
The Night Is Mine
I Own the Dawn
Wait Until Dark
Take Over at Midnight
Light Up the Night
Bring On the Dusk
By Break of Day

AND THE NAVY
Christmas at Steel Beach
Christmas at Peleliu Cove

WHITE HOUSE HOLIDAY
*Daniel's Christmas**
*Frank's Independence Day**
*Peter's Christmas**
*Zachary's Christmas**
*Roy's Independence Day**
*Damien's Christmas**

5E
Target of the Heart
Target Lock on Love
Target of Mine
Target of One's Own

Shadow Force: Psi
*At the Slightest Sound**
*At the Quietest Word**

White House Protection Force
*Off the Leash**
*On Your Mark**
*In the Weeds**

Contemporary Romance

Eagle Cove
Return to Eagle Cove
Recipe for Eagle Cove
Longing for Eagle Cove
Keepsake for Eagle Cove

Henderson's Ranch
*Nathan's Big Sky**
*Big Sky, Loyal Heart**
*Big Sky Dog Whisperer**

Love Abroad
Heart of the Cotswolds: England
Path of Love: Cinque Terre, Italy

Other works by M. L. Buchman:

Contemporary Romance (cont)

Where Dreams
Where Dreams are Born
Where Dreams Reside
Where Dreams Are of Christmas
Where Dreams Unfold
Where Dreams Are Written

Science Fiction / Fantasy

Deities Anonymous
Cookbook from Hell: Reheated
Saviors 101

Single Titles
The Nara Reaction
Monk's Maze
the Me and Elsie Chronicles

Non-Fiction

Strategies for Success
Managing Your Inner Artist/Writer
Estate Planning for Authors
Character Voice

Short Story Series by M. L. Buchman:

Romantic Suspense

Delta Force
Delta Force

Firehawks
The Firehawks Lookouts
The Firehawks Hotshots
The Firebirds

The Night Stalkers
The Night Stalkers
The Night Stalkers 5E
The Night Stalkers CSAR
The Night Stalkers Wedding Stories

US Coast Guard
US Coast Guard

White House Protection Force
White House Protection Force

Contemporary Romance

Eagle Cove
Eagle Cove

Henderson's Ranch
Henderson's Ranch

Where Dreams
Where Dreams

Thrillers

Dead Chef
Dead Chef

Science Fiction / Fantasy

Deities Anonymous
Deities Anonymous

Other
The Future Night Stalkers
Single Titles

SIGN UP FOR M. L. BUCHMAN'S NEWSLETTER TODAY

and receive:
Release News
Free Short Stories
a Free Book

Get your free book today. Do it now.
free-book.mlbuchman.com